THE BACHELOR'S BABY SURPRISE

TERI WILSON

For Cameron

Chapter One

"Come quickly... I am tasting stars."
—*Dom Pérignon, at his first sip of champagne*

Evangeline Holly was no stranger to guilty pleasures.

Like Audrey Hepburn, she had a fondness for a nice creamy chocolate cake. In fact, she was on a first-name basis with most everyone at Magnolia Bakery's Bleecker Street location in Greenwich Village.

She was also currently housing not just one, but *two* special-needs Cavalier King Charles spaniels in her very tiny, very *non*-pet-friendly apartment. So yeah. She had her vices.

But she also knew where and when to draw the line. Evangeline knew her limits. And for her, those limits included two noteworthy things she'd never once indulged in—bad wine and one-night stands.

Until now.

Her head throbbed. She dragged her eyelids open, and the first thing her gaze landed on was her pair of dogs snoring madly atop a man's Armani suit jacket that had been discarded on the bedroom floor. Beside it, a pair of trousers and a crisp white Oxford shirt rested in a heap.

Okay then.

She closed her eyes and reminded herself that there wasn't anything inherently wrong with cheap wine or casual sex. It was just that growing up on a vineyard in Upstate New York simply precluded her from experiencing the former. If she was a wine snob, she'd at least come by it honestly.

As for the latter...

Chalk that up to being involved in a devoted, monogamous relationship with the same man for most of her adult life. Also, no one actually had time for intimacy these days, did they? Evangeline had never quite believed everyone was spending as much time in bed as they cheekily hinted at.

She opened her eyes again. Early morning sunlight glinted off the pair of cuff links on her nightstand. There were *cuff links* on her nightstand. Cuff links from Tiffany & Co., but still.

She'd been wrong about everything. So. Very. Wrong.

Most notably the assumption that her relationship was in any way devoted. Or monogamous. On her end, yes. On Jeremy's, not so much. Apparently, he'd been spending plenty of time in bed…with his sous chef. Not Evangeline.

She'd been enlightened three days ago. It was startling how much could change in three measly days. She'd lost her boyfriend. She'd lost her job. Basic truths she'd believed about her life had gone right out the window.

As had Evangeline's previous avoidance of certain weaknesses.

The pounding in her head was a testament that she'd broken her *no bad wine* rule the night before. The evidence of her first-ever one-night stand was far more tangible—from the clothes and the cuff links to the startlingly attractive man lying beside her with his eyes closed, dressed in nothing but her nicest bedsheets.

"Good morning." He spoke without opening his eyes, as if he could sense her staring at him. His voice was delicious, low and unfamiliar. Not at all like Jeremy's.

"Um." She swallowed. What had she been thinking? She'd brought a complete stranger back to her apartment, and here he was. Naked in her bed.

She blamed Jeremy. This was 90 percent his fault. The other ten percent of the blame fell squarely on the shoulders of the pinot grigio she could still taste in the back of her throat. *Pinot grigio*, for God's sake.

"Good morning," she finally said, even though nothing about it seemed good.

She didn't know what to say or how to act. She wasn't even sure where to look, although she couldn't seem to force her gaze away from the owner of the cuff links. He stretched and rolled onto his back, giving her an eyeful of taut male skin and finely sculpted abdominal muscles.

Her throat grew dry. Where on earth had she found this beautiful person? And how had she summoned up the nerve to flirt with him? Flirting must have happened at some point for him to end up here, right?

Jeremy's voice rose up from the pinot-drenched fog in her mind. *Of course I've been sleeping around. What did you expect? You're not exactly a sexual person, Evangeline. I just need more.* Most *people need more.*

So that's how she'd found the courage. When your boyfriend insinuated you were terrible in bed, you either curled up into a ball or went about proving him wrong. Two days in the fetal position had been more than enough.

The sound of a deeply male throat clearing dragged her back to the present.

Evangeline's gaze flitted from the stranger's trim waist to his drowsy half grin. He'd caught her ogling him. Perfect.

Her face went hot. "Look, um…"

"Ryan," he said, tucking his arms behind his head, causing the sheet to dip even lower.

Don't look. Do. Not.

She looked, and a sultry warmth washed over her, settling in the very same areas that Jeremy had called dead just three days prior.

"Right." She bit her lip and met his gaze again. "Ryan. I knew that."

"I believe you." He winked. Clearly he didn't, even though Ryan had been the first name that came to her once she'd spotted the *RW* engraved on his cuff links. "Eve."

Eve?

No one had ever called her Eve. Always Evangeline.

She remembered hearing somewhere that *Eve* meant *living*. She tried not to think too hard about that while there was a naked man named Ryan with the body of a Greek god stretched out beside her. "Anyway, *Ryan*, what I'm trying to say is that I don't typically do this sort of thing."

"Yes, I know. You mentioned that last night. A couple of times, actually." He rested a warm hand on her upper thigh and gave her a smile that seemed a bit sad around the edges. Bittersweet.

She felt oddly transparent, as if the man in her bed knew more about her than was possible after only a handful of hours together. Her thigh was suddenly awash in goose bumps.

"Good. So long as we're clear—this was a one-night affair. A mistake, probably. I don't expect you to ask for my number or anything." She slid her leg out of reach, tucking it beneath the covers.

His smile faded. The dimples which had been barely visible beneath the layer of scruff on his chiseled jaw disappeared entirely. "A mistake?"

She nodded, because of course it had been a mistake.

A man was the very last thing she needed, even for one night. Particularly *this* man, whose hands she couldn't look at without imagining them on her skin. And whose mouth made her want to linger in bed and revisit the most wicked portions of the previous evening. "Good grief, how much wine did I have last night?"

She clamped her mouth closed. God, had she actually asked that question out loud?

"Quite a bit." Ryan's frown deepened. She couldn't stop saying his name in her head. *Ryan. Ryan. Ryan.* "Although you didn't seem drunk. Not even tipsy. Should I be apologizing right now? Something tells me I should."

Another perk of having a vineyard in your childhood backyard—an incredibly high tolerance. For wine, at least. Even on the rare occasion when she drank enough to *feel* like she'd overindulged, it never showed.

"You have nothing to apologize for. Truly." Memories flitted through her consciousness. The taste of him. The feel of him. The weight of him on top of her as he'd pushed himself inside.

It had been exactly what she'd wanted.

Exquisite.

A shiver coursed through her, and she leaped out of the bed to prevent herself from reaching for him again.

Ryan's gaze settled on her, and she felt it as keenly as if it were a caress. Her thoughts screamed. *Ryan. Ryan. Ryan.* She'd cried out his name last night, hadn't she?

Oh God.

She crossed her arms, and his gaze drifted lower, lingering on her bare breasts. She was every bit as naked as he was, which made perfect sense, given the situation. She'd just been so preoccupied with *his* nakedness that she hadn't noticed her own.

"What if I *wanted* to ask for your number?" he said, making no move whatsoever to evacuate her bed.

How long was he planning on staying? Did Ryan not realize how one-night stands worked?

Ryan. Ryan. Ryan.

Evangeline had repeated the name to herself so many times now that it no longer made sense. She wondered what the *W* on the cuff links stood for, but she didn't dare ask. If she knew his full name, she might be tempted to look him up later in another moment of weakness.

Not happening.

She grabbed the quilt off the end of the bed, wrapped it around herself and shook her head. "You don't want my number."

A muscle flicked in his jaw. "I'm certain I do."

"No." She shook her head even harder. "You don't."

If he knew the first thing about her situation, he'd run for the hills. She wouldn't blame him in the slightest.

"Then I must be an idiot," he said.

Did he have to be so charming? He probably couldn't help it. It was probably part of his genetic makeup, like the abs. And the voice. And the fathomless blue of his eyes.

Evangeline had never seen eyes quite so blue.

She averted her gaze from them.

"Honestly, you don't need to do this. Everything's fine. I'm fine. This was—" *Just what I needed.* She swallowed around the lump that had formed in her throat, seemingly out of nowhere "—fun."

"Fun," he echoed.

The word sounded oddly hollow, and Evangeline instantly wanted to take it back. She had to bite the inside of her cheek to stop herself from telling him the whole truth—that she was lost; she'd been lost for a very long time and that the real reason she never did this sort of thing was because it scared the life out of her.

Intimacy, in all its forms, involved a level of vulnerability that she couldn't quite handle. She thought Jeremy had understood that about her. Wrong again.

"Here you go, then." She bent to retrieve his abandoned shirt and trousers and handed them to him. When his fingertips brushed against hers, the lump in her throat doubled in size.

Leave. Please, leave.

He climbed out of the bed and started to get dressed. Thank goodness.

She glanced at the floor, where Olive and Bee were still sound asleep on top of Ryan's suit jacket. Olive's paws twitched. She was chasing rabbits in her sleep again.

Evangeline tugged gently on the wool Armani, trying her hardest to slip it out from beneath the sleeping dogs unnoticed. Like the old magician's tablecloth trick.

No such luck. Bee was completely deaf, therefore extremely sensitive to movement. She woke with a start, pawing at Evangeline's shins. Olive let out a squeaky dog yawn and hopped onto the bed, where she stood and stared at Ryan while he zipped up his pants.

He glanced up, spotted Olive watching him and then reached to scratch behind her ears.

"Pet her from the left side. She can't see out of her right eye, so you might startle her," Evangeline said.

He followed her advice. The little Cavalier's tail wagged furiously. Bee scrambled up onto the bed to join in the fun.

"Sweet dogs," Ryan said, and Evangeline's heart gave a little tug.

He somehow managed to look even more attractive, surrounded by adorable dogs. Because of course.

"Thank you. They technically belong to my grandfather, but he recently moved into an extended care facility, so they live here now." Why was she telling him this?

"I'm sorry to hear that." His voice went as soft as velvet, like he really meant it.

If he didn't leave soon, she'd probably offer to cook him breakfast.

"Here." She shoved his suit jacket at him. Every inch of it was covered in dog hair.

He pretended not to notice and slid it on, anyway. And that small act of kindness was almost more than she could bear. Maybe last night hadn't been a mistake after all. Maybe the mistake was happening right now.

Maybe she shouldn't be in such a hurry to let him go.

"Goodbye, then," she said in as firm a voice as she could manage.

He came around the bed, and when he was an arm's length away, he lifted his hand as if to cup her face. She took a tiny backward step.

His hand fell to his side. "Goodbye, Eve."

And then he was gone.

* * *

Ryan Wilde stood outside Eve's apartment and watched as the door shut in his face.

Well, he thought, *that was different.*

He'd never been so summarily tossed out of a woman's bed before. Then again, he typically didn't make a habit out of bedding women he didn't actually know.

Especially lately.

Ryan's love life had been rather complicated in recent weeks, thanks to the *New York Times*. He'd been doing his best to avoid romantic entanglements altogether.

He walked down the hall, making his way to the building's front steps and pulled his cell phone from the inside pocket of his suit jacket—which looked more like a fur coat at the moment—and rang the Bennington Hotel's driver.

The chauffeur answered on the first ring. "Mr. Wilde, how can I help you?"

Ryan didn't often take advantage of the more luxurious perks that came with being chief financial officer of the Bennington, but having a driver on standby was nice at a time like this. He glanced up and down the picturesque street. The sun was just coming up, bathing the neighborhood brownstones in soft winter hues of violet and blue. The snowy sidewalks were empty, save for an older man opening up the newsstand on the corner. "Are you free to come pick me up in the Village?"

He was, of course. Who needed a limo this time of day?

Ryan gave the driver his location, then pocketed his phone again. He rubbed his hands together. His breath was a visible puff of vapor in the crisp air. What the hell had he done with his coat?

He lifted his gaze to the row of windows on the third floor, trying to guess which one was Eve's. He wished he'd left his Burberry trench up there so he'd have a legitimate excuse to see her again, but he hadn't. He'd left it on the back of a chair at the wine bar the night before—forgotten, completely—right around the time he'd spotted Eve across the room, brandishing a butcher knife.

It had been one of the most bizarre things he'd ever seen. She'd grabbed a bottle of champagne and before he'd been able to process what he was seeing, she severed the neck of the bottle with the knife. Sliced it clean off, just below the cork. It made a loud popping sound, and she'd stood there with a quiet smile on her face while bubbles spilled down her arm. The group of people at her table cheered. All men, he'd noticed.

She wasn't on a date, though, from what he could tell. The table was piled with note cards, as if they were some kind of study group.

Note cards. In the middle of a wine bar on Friday night.

"That was quite the party trick," Ryan had said after he'd abandoned his coat, his drink and the trio of business associates he'd been meeting with.

He'd had to talk to her. *Had* to.

For the better part of a week, he'd been avoiding every marriage-minded single woman in Manhattan. But the knife-wielding goddess had gotten under his skin instantly. He wasn't even sure why.

Yes, she was pretty. More than pretty, actually.

Beautiful, with full red lips and long, spun-gold hair—the kind of hair that made him hard just thinking about what it would feel like sliding through his fingers.

But it had been more than her looks that had him spellbound from all the way across the crowded room. He'd felt an inexplicable pull deep in his chest when he looked at her. And as he came closer, there'd been something else. She'd had secrets in her eyes.

"It's not a party trick," she'd said, looking him up and down. A scarlet flush made its way up her porcelain face. "It's called sabering."

She'd gone on to explain that French cavalry officers had used their swords in a similar manner to open champagne during the Napoleonic Wars. Which didn't explain in the slightest why she was doing it in a wine bar on the Upper West Side, but Ryan hadn't cared.

It had fascinated him. *She'd* fascinated him…

Fascinated him enough that he very purposefully neglected to mention his last name.

A car rounded the corner. Ryan turned in the direction of the sound of tires crunching on packed snow, but it wasn't the Bennington limo. Where was the damned thing? He was freezing.

He bowed his head against the wind and walked toward the newsstand, hoping the old man could sell him some coffee.

He felt bad about the name thing, even now. Even after she'd shown him the door within minutes of waking up in her bed. It wasn't as if he'd lied to her. He'd just left off his surname.

Call me Ryan.

Thinking about that made him wince. It made him sound like a player, when in actuality, he was anything but.

That was the big irony of his current situation. Practically overnight, and through no fault of his own, he'd developed a *reputation*. A reputation that had no basis in reality.

It had been a relief when he realized Eve had no idea who he was.

Eve, with her butcher knife and lovely head full of history.

"Excuse me," he said.

The man behind the newsstand looked up. "Yeah?"

"Have you got any coffee back there?"

The man nodded. "Sure do. Extra hot."

"Perfect." Ryan opened his wallet and removed a few bills. As he handed the old man the money, his gaze snagged on a magazine.

Gotham. But the title didn't matter. It was the image on the magazine's cover that gave him pause.

A man's face.

His face.

If Evangeline Holly hadn't known who he was last night, she would now.

Chapter Two

Six weeks later

Ryan was late.

In the three years since he'd been named CFO of the Bennington, he'd been the first member of the executive staff to arrive for work every morning. He was notorious for it.

Sometimes the chief executive officer purposely tried to get there first, just to get under Ryan's skin. But Ryan had a sixth sense when it came to predicting moves like that, probably because Zander Wilde wasn't just the CEO. He was also Ryan's cousin. The two men had known each other a lifetime. Ryan knew Zander like a brother.

Consequently, he wasn't the least bit shocked to find Zander waiting for him when he strode into his office five minutes later than his usual arrival time. Annoyed, yes. Shocked, not so much.

"Well, well, well. Look what the cat dragged in." Zander was reclining in Ryan's chair with his feet resting on the smooth mahogany surface of his desk, ankles crossed. He folded the newspaper in his hands and shot Ryan a triumphant grin. "Looks like I got here first."

Ryan set his briefcase down and lowered himself into one of his office guest chairs. "Pleased with yourself?"

Zander's smile widened. "I am, actually."

"Enjoy your victory." Ryan lifted a brow. "Especially since it was three years in the making."

Zander shrugged. "I'll take it. A win is a win."

"If you say so, but would it kill you to get your feet off my desk?" He glared at his cousin's wing tips.

Zander rolled his eyes before planting his feet on the floor and sitting up straight. "I need to talk to you about something. But first, what's wrong? You're not dying or terminally ill, are you? You're never late."

"It's 7:35 a.m.," Ryan said flatly.

Zander's only response was a blank stare.

"I'm not dying. I was just…" He cleared his throat. "Delayed."

"Delayed?" Zander smirked. "I get it now. This is a bachelor-specific problem."

He cast a pointed glance at the framed magazine cover hanging above the desk. Gotham Names Ryan Wilde New York's Hottest Bachelor of the Year, the headline screamed.

Six weeks had passed since Ryan had learned about his "coronation," as Zander liked to put it. His feelings about the matter had remained unchanged since that snowy morning at the newsstand in the West Village. Namely, he loathed it.

He especially loathed seeing the magazine cover on the wall of his office every day, but it was preferable to having it on display in the Bennington lobby, where Zander had originally hung it. Ryan suspected it had been a joke and his cousin had never intended to leave it there, but he wasn't taking any chances. The terms of their compromise dictated that the framed piece made its home on the wall above Ryan's desk.

Oh joy.

"Let me guess." Zander narrowed his gaze. "You were out late last night fighting women off with a stick."

Hardly.

Ryan hadn't indulged in female company for weeks. *Six* weeks, in fact. Although his recent abstinence wasn't altogether related to the *Gotham* feature article.

He couldn't seem to get Evangeline Holly out of his head. A couple of times, he'd even gone so far as to visit her building in the Village. He'd lingered on the front steps for a few minutes, thinking about their night together.

It had been good.

Better than good.

It had been spectacular, damn it. The best sex of his life, which was reason enough to let it go and move on. That kind of magic only came along once. Any attempt to recreate it would have been in vain.

Maybe not, though. Maybe the night hadn't been magical at all. Maybe *she'd* been the magic.

He'd considered this both times he'd nearly knocked on her door. Then he'd remembered how eager she'd been to get rid of him on the morning after, and he'd come to his senses. The woman had refused to give him her phone number. That seemed like a pretty solid indication that she would've been less than thrilled to find him knocking on her door.

"I watched the Rangers game and then went to bed," he said. Then for added emphasis, "Alone."

"So what gives? Why are you late?" Zander frowned. "Wait. Don't tell me the groupies are back."

Ryan wanted to correct him. The groupies weren't technically back, because they'd never gone away. They'd been hanging around the Bennington for nearly two months—since the day the *New York Times* had decided to throw a wrench in his otherwise peaceful life.

He should have seen it coming. The Bennington had been the subject of a wildly popular series of columns in the *Times'* Weddings page. A reporter for the Vows column had speculated that the hotel was cursed after several weddings in the Bennington ballroom had ended like a scene from *Runaway Bride*.

But that was ancient history.

Should have been, anyway. Ryan had negotiated a cease-fire with the reporter. In exchange for exclusive coverage of Zander's recent nuptials, the reporter declared the curse over and done with. But Ryan hadn't anticipated that the last line of her column would imply he was on the lookout for a bride himself.

It had been brief—just a single sentence. But that handful of words had been enough. Women had been throwing themselves at him in a steady stream—

morning, noon and night. His photo on the cover of *Gotham* had only made things worse.

Ryan sighed. "There are half a dozen of them waiting for me in the lobby. I had to go around the block and come in through the service entrance in the back."

"You *had* to?" Zander let out a snort. "Here's an idea. Call me crazy, but why don't you go to the lobby right now, talk to the lovely ladies and ask one of them out on a date?"

He couldn't be serious. "Absolutely not."

Those women knew nothing about him, other than the fact that he was single. And rich. It didn't take a genius to know why they wanted to marry him, a total stranger.

No, thank you. He'd nearly been married once already, and once was enough. Never again.

Zander rolled his eyes. "You realize almost every man in New York would trade places with you in a heartbeat right now, don't you?"

"Is that so?" Ryan crossed his arms. "You wouldn't."

"Of course I wouldn't. I'm a happily married newlywed."

Precisely.

Ryan was thrilled for Zander. He really was. But that didn't mean he was going to pick a woman at random from the marriage-minded crowd in the lobby. This wasn't an episode of *The Bachelor*. This was his life.

"Good for you. I prefer my dalliances more temporary. Short-term and strings-free. Can we talk about something else now?" *Anything* else. "You said you needed to speak to me. I trust it's about something other than my personal life."

"It is." Zander picked up his discarded newspaper, spread it open and slid it across the desk toward Ryan. "Have you seen this?"

He glanced down. The *New York Times*. Not his favorite media outlet of late, for obvious reasons.

At least it wasn't open to the Weddings page.

"The food section?" Surely he hadn't merited a mention in one of the cuisine columns. "No, I haven't."

"The restaurant column contains an interesting tidbit. Right here." Zander indicated a paragraph halfway down the page.

Ryan scanned it.

Carlo Bocci was spotted checking into the Plaza last night, fueling rumors that he's in town for his annual month-long restaurant tour on behalf of the *Michelin Guide*. This time last year, Mr. Bocci visited a total of thirty-five New York eateries, ultimately bestowing the coveted Michelin star on fewer than ten. Only one of those restaurants, The White Swan, was awarded three Michelin stars, the highest possible ranking. The White Swan was recently named America's finest restaurant by *Food & Wine* magazine.

He looked up. "Let me guess. We're upset that he's staying at the Plaza instead of the Bennington."

"No. It doesn't matter where he stays. What matters is…"

Ryan finished for him. "The Michelin stars."

"Precisely." Zander's mouth hitched into a half grin. "Do you have any idea what a three-star Michelin ranking for Bennington 8 would mean?"

Bennington 8, the hotel's premiere fine dining restaurant, was located in the rooftop atrium. With its sweeping views of Manhattan, it already performed remarkably well as far as bookings went. But three Michelin stars would keep their reservations calendar full six months out.

It would mean money.

A lot of money.

An *obscene* amount of money.

The Bennington could use that kind of income since the runaway bride curse had put a serious dent in their cash flow. They were bouncing back, but not fast enough.

Ryan frowned and smoothed down his tie. "Three stars? Do you really think that's doable?"

They didn't even know if Bennington 8 was on Carlo Bocci's review list. The list was secret. Ryan suspected he booked his reservations under an assumed name and showed up when least expected, as most restaurant reviewers did.

Zander shook his head. "No, not the way we stand at the moment. Which is why you and I will be in interviews all afternoon today and tomorrow. As long as it takes."

"You want to hire a new chef? I'm not sure that's a wise idea." The chef they had was one of the best in the city. They'd never get anyone else of his caliber on such short notice, much less someone better.

"Agreed. Patrick is as good as we're going to get.

As far as food is concerned, we're golden. But that's only half the battle, isn't it?"

Ryan glanced back down at the newspaper and his gaze zeroed in on three italicized words—*Food & Wine* magazine.

"Wine," Ryan said, nodding slowly. "You want to hire a sommelier."

"A wine director—someone with impeccable credentials. Without a good somm, we haven't got a chance. Have we got room in the budget to hire someone?"

"I'll make room." He'd be staring at spreadsheets all day, trying to make it work. But that was fine. Numbers were Ryan's specialty. There were no gray areas with numerical figures, only black and white.

Just the way Ryan liked it.

Zander stood, folded the copy of the *Times* and tucked it under his arm. "Great. I've already put out some feelers. I'll start lining up interviews. Clear your calendar."

"Done." Ryan rounded the desk and reclaimed his seat.

Zander lingered in the doorway. "Let's hope we find someone immediately. This could be tough, but surely there's an out-of-work somm somewhere in the city who's also charismatic enough to impress Bocci."

Ryan's thoughts flitted back to six weeks ago. To a little wine bar in the Village. To Evangeline Holly, her butcher knife and the way her lips had tasted of warm grapes, fresh from the vine.

He pushed the memory away.

Zander was asking the impossible, but Ryan was

grateful for the challenge. He needed to get his focus back. He needed to forget about the numerous women who wanted to marry him. He especially needed to forget about the one who *didn't*.

He shot Zander a look of grim determination. "If the right person is out there, trust me, we'll find 'em."

Evangeline was getting desperate.

If she was being honest with herself—truly, *brutally* honest—she'd passed the point of desperation a few days ago.

Six weeks was a long time to go without a paycheck, especially when she was already contributing more than she could afford to her grandfather's care.

Maybe she'd been impulsive.

So she and Jeremy had broken up. So he'd been sleeping with his sous chef. Did that really mean Evangeline couldn't stay on at the restaurant?

Of course that's what it means. Are you insane? Don't even think about crawling back.

She lifted her chin and marched through the revolving doors of the Bennington Hotel.

She had to get this job. If she didn't, crawling back to Jeremy was exactly what she'd be forced to do by day's end.

"Can I help you?" The woman behind the reception desk gazed impassively at her.

"Yes, I'm here for an interview. I have an appointment at four o'clock." Evangeline forced a smile and tightened her grip on her Everlane tote bag—a leftover luxury from her previous life.

It was startling how much things could change in

a month and a half. She'd thought she'd had everything figured out. She'd been happy.

At least she'd thought she had been happy. Now she wasn't so sure.

You were *happy. You were perfectly content with Jeremy. Stop thinking about* that *night.*

She swallowed. The one-night stand was still messing with her head, six weeks after the fact. Which was all the proof she needed that one-night stands were *not* her thing. Lesson learned.

In the days since she'd woken up to the sight of those unfamiliar cuff links on her bedside table and the outrageously handsome man in her bed, she'd questioned nearly everything about her past relationship and life in general.

How was it possible to feel such an intense connection with someone she'd only just met? She'd gone to bed with the man, and she hadn't even known his last name.

She knew it now, though. Wilde. Ryan Wilde. It was kind of hard not to notice his name and face on every newsstand in Manhattan. *Gotham* magazine had named him New York's hottest bachelor or something ridiculous like that.

Of course. No wonder she'd been so charmed by him. There hadn't actually been anything special about their night together. He was just really, really good at sex. He probably couldn't even help it. It was an occupational hazard of being the city's biggest playboy.

Out of all the men in Manhattan, she'd fallen into bed with *him*. She was so mortified that she hadn't even bought the magazine with his face on the cover. She wanted to forget that night had ever happened.

Unfortunately, she couldn't. It was too damned memorable.

She blushed every time she thought about it, and she'd spent far too long trying to figure out why she'd never felt so passionate in bed with Jeremy.

So maybe she hadn't been as happy with him as she'd thought. Clearly she'd been wrong about things. *A lot* of things.

But she'd at least been on the verge of having her dream job handed to her on a silver platter. And now...

Now here she was, applying for a position she was in no way qualified for. Her only hope was that the Bennington Hotel was every bit as desperate as she was.

"Have a seat, Miss Holly. The general manager will be with you in just a moment." The woman behind the reception desk motioned toward one of the lobby's plush velvet sofas, situated beneath a glittering crystal chandelier.

"Thank you." Evangeline flashed another smile and headed across the marble floor.

She could do this. The hotel was, in fact, desperate. At least that's what Colin, one of the study partners in her wine group, had told her when he called to tell her about the job opening. They needed a sommelier, and they needed one fast.

Surely all the best somms in Manhattan were already employed. Evangeline hoped so. If she had to compete for this job against even one sommelier with actual credentials, she was toast.

"Hello," she said to the three other women sitting in the waiting area. Her competition, she assumed.

Odd.

Most sommeliers were men, particularly the ones who held wine director titles. At the highest certified level—master sommelier—men claimed 85 percent of the spots.

All three women swiveled their gazes in Evangeline's direction, but none of them returned the greeting. The one closest to her—a glossy brunette wearing a blouse that seemed far too low-cut to be considered professional—looked her up and down and finally spoke.

"Interesting, but I doubt you're his type." She sniffed and crossed one tawny leg over the other.

"I beg your pardon," Evangeline said.

His *type*?

Whose type?

And what kind of pervy work environment was this?

The brunette shrugged. "Just a hunch. There are a lot of us. It's going to take more than a tasteful pencil skirt and a red lip to stand out."

Evangeline blinked and fought the urge to flee.

Don't let her get to you. You know wine. She's probably trying to psych you out.

It was working. She was desperate, but not desperate enough to use her cleavage to make an impression.

What am I doing here?

She should have known this opportunity was too good to be true.

She stood, ready to bolt, but someone called her name before she could take a step.

"Miss Holly?" A man in a dark suit extended his hand. "I'm Elliot Ross, the general manager. We spoke on the phone earlier this morning."

She shook his hand, relief coursing through her when he kept his gaze firmly focused on her eyes. Not her pencil skirt. "Pleased to meet you."

The other women were no longer paying her any attention whatsoever. Things were getting weirder by the minute.

"The CEO and CFO are conducting the interviews upstairs in the restaurant. If you'll come with me, we'll get things underway." Elliot Ross waved her toward the shiny gold elevator doors.

Evangeline followed.

Once inside the elevator, he pushed the button marked Rooftop. "We appreciate your willingness to come on such short notice. The CEO is keen to fill this position as soon as possible."

Thank goodness. "I'm available to start right away."

"Excellent. You're the last of the candidates to be interviewed this afternoon, and I'm afraid I neglected to include your name on the list. Do you have a résumé?"

She'd hoped to avoid having to talk about her qualifications. A pipe dream, obviously. Couldn't she just talk about wine? She was good at that, regardless of what her résumé indicated.

"Here." She handed him a copy of her qualifications, minimal as they were.

Shake it off. This job is perfect for you.

Then the elevator doors swung open, and Evangeline realized she had something much more important to worry about than her lack of experience. Correction: some*one*.

Someone who'd been naked in her bed the last time she'd seen him, unless spotting his face on all those magazine covers counted.

Someone named Ryan Wilde.

Chapter Three

What was happening?

What was Ryan Wilde, her one-night stand, doing at her job interview—the most important job interview she'd ever had?

"Miss Holly, thank you for coming." Another man—the only man in the room she *hadn't* slept with—had spoken. She'd nearly forgotten he was there. Every bit of awareness in her body was focused squarely on Ryan. "I'm Zander Wilde, CEO of the Bennington."

"It's lovely to meet you," she said.

At least that's what she thought she said. She wasn't sure what words were actually coming out of her mouth.

Zander cleared his throat, and Evangeline realized she wasn't even looking at him. He was talking to her, and she was staring right past him, fixated on Ryan.

She couldn't seem to tear her gaze away from Ryan's chiseled face. He seemed even more handsome than she remembered. How was that possible? She swallowed—hard—and tried to figure out what was different about him.

He was a bit cleaner cut, for one thing. The dark scruff that had lined his jaw the last time she'd seen him was gone. Naturally. He'd probably woken up in his own bed, in his own apartment, where he'd shaved with his own razor.

He was also wearing glasses, which unfortunately failed to lessen the effect of his dreamy blue eyes. In fact, they looked even bluer behind the square cut black frames. Forget-me-not blue.

Zander cleared his throat again, louder this time. "Do you two know each other?"

"No," she blurted.

Ryan simultaneously said, "Yes, we do."

Zander glanced back and forth between them. "Which is it? Yes or no?"

She'd just told a bald-faced lie. The interview was off to a stellar start.

"Actually..." She took a deep breath and tried to figure out a way to change her answer that wouldn't make her sound like a crazy person.

"Actually, it seems I'm mistaken," Ryan said smoothly. "We don't know one another. Forgive me... Miss Holly, is it?"

He offered her his hand, and she had no choice but to take it.

"Yes, that's correct." Her voice sounded breathier

than it should have, and she couldn't make herself let go of his hand.

It was warm. Familiar. And when she looked down at the place where his fingertips brushed against her skin, all she could think about was the pad of his thumb dragging softly, slowly against the swell of her bottom lip.

Let go! Let go of his hand.

She dropped it like a hot potato and turned to face Zander. "I'm assuming the wine director reports to you since you're the CEO."

Ryan couldn't be her boss. No way.

Not that she'd gotten the job yet. Her chances were slim to none. Colin had mentioned they'd interviewed a master sommelier. Less than two hundred people in the world held that title. And presumably none of them had had sex with Ryan Wilde.

Zander's gaze narrowed. "Technically, the position reports to the CEO. But the wine director will work closely with the CFO, particularly with regard to the wine budget. So I suppose a certain amount of compatibility is important."

"Compatibility." Evangeline's gaze flitted toward Ryan, and he sent her a nearly imperceptible wink. She wanted to die. "Right."

"Shall we proceed?" Zander motioned toward a table in the center of the room.

"Absolutely." She did her best to ignore the way her knees went wobbly as she crossed the vast space and took a seat.

So it had come to this?

After a six-week-long job search, her only choices

were working for the man who'd dumped her or drawing up wine budgets with her one-night stand?

Lovely.

Also ironic, considering she'd so recently been accused of being an ice queen.

But she was getting ahead of herself, wasn't she? She hadn't been offered the job at Bennington 8 yet, and at the rate things were going, she wouldn't be.

She lifted her chin, met Zander's gaze across the table and decided to pretend Ryan wasn't even there. "The atmosphere here is stunning."

"Thank you," Zander said and glanced up at the glass dome ceiling overhead.

Snow fell softly against the atrium, and the twinkling lights of Manhattan glittered against the darkening sky. The interior of the restaurant was the epitome of cool winter elegance, with crisp white linens and pale blue velvet chairs. Evangeline felt like she was sitting inside a snow globe—trapped inside a perfect world, immune to the swirling chaos outside.

She took a deep breath and gave the snow globe a good, hard shake. "But your wine list is weak at best."

Ryan let out a quiet laugh, reminding her that he was still there, sitting beside her. She allowed herself a quick glance at him.

He arched a brow.

She kept her expression as neutral as possible and redirected her gaze at Zander.

A muscle flicked in his jaw. "Interesting. The other candidates didn't seem to think so."

"Are you sure? Or were they simply trying to flatter you?" She smiled sweetly at him. "I won't do that."

"Clearly," he muttered.

"But that means you can trust me to give you my honest opinion. And my opinion of your current list is that it's not good enough." She swallowed. If she didn't get the job, she'd at least make an impression.

Impressions were important. Being a sommelier was about more than choosing wine. It was about service. A good somm made drinking a glass of wine a memorable experience. There was an art to talking about wine and presenting a bottle—to opening it and pouring its contents.

People often overlooked that part of the job, and it was Evangeline's biggest strength.

"How would you change the list?" Zander said.

She was ready for this. Bennington 8's wine list was listed on its website, and she'd committed it to memory.

"For starters, I'd eliminate the pinot grigio. There are far better light-bodied whites." She studiously avoided Ryan's gaze, since it was apparently his wine of choice.

Then she told herself she was being ridiculous. He probably didn't even remember ordering multiple bottles of it all those weeks ago.

He laughed—with just a little too much force— and when she ventured a glance in his direction, the smirk on his face told her that his memory of their night together was just as intact as hers was.

Her face went hot, and she looked away.

"What else?" Zander asked, leaning forward in his chair. "Do enlighten us."

"I'd cut your California wines by two-thirds.

You've only got three old-world wines on your list. That's unacceptable."

"How so?" Ryan said.

"Wine is about history. The Roman army didn't march on water. Roman soldiers marched on wine. A good old-world wine lets you experience the past as you drink it. You can taste everything—the earth, the rivers, the sunshine of centuries. There's nothing quite so beautiful."

Ryan and Zander exchanged a look that Evangeline wasn't sure how to interpret. She was either nailing it, or she sounded delusional. There was no hiding the fact that she was a wine nerd of the highest order.

"I'm sure most of your customers walk in here asking for wines from Napa Valley and Sonoma, California, or the Finger Lakes region upstate because that's what they're familiar with." She shrugged. "They don't know what they're missing. That's why you need a wine expert."

Zander glanced down at the sheet of paper on the table in front of him. "But I'm looking at your résumé, and there's no mention of a sommelier certificate of any sort."

Here we go.

This was where each and every one of her other interviews had gone south. Way south.

"I'm self-taught. My family owns a vineyard upstate." *Not anymore, remember?* She blinked and corrected herself. "Owned."

Ryan's gaze narrowed ever so slightly, and she felt nearly as exposed as she'd been the last time they'd stood in the same room together.

She took a deep breath. "I'm studying for the certification exam, though. I should be prepared to take it when it's offered next April."

Zander frowned. "That's several months from now."

"Yes, I know." She smiled, but neither of the men met her gaze. Not even Ryan.

She needed to do something. Fast.

"Let me open a bottle for you," she blurted. "Please."

Zander glanced at his watch, which was pretty much the universal sign that time was up. The interview was over. "I don't think—"

Ryan cut him off. "Let her do it."

Evangeline felt like kissing him all of a sudden. Not that the thought hadn't already crossed her mind. This time, though, she had to physically stop herself from popping out of her chair and kissing him smack on the lips.

"Excellent. Why don't you point me in the direction of your wine cooler, and I'll select a bottle?" She stood before Zander could argue.

His gaze swiveled back and forth between her and Ryan again, just like when they'd given opposite answers to his question about whether they knew one another.

He knows. It was probably written all over her face. *News flash: I slept with your cousin.*

Was there a woman in Manhattan whom Ryan Wilde *hadn't* slept with? That was the real question.

"Very well." Zander waved a hand, and the hotel's general manager appeared out of nowhere. "Show Miss Holly to the wine cooler, please. And bring her a corkscrew."

She smiled. "Oh, I won't need a corkscrew."

* * *

Ryan watched as Evangeline studied the wines lined up on their sides in the cooler on the far side of the restaurant. He knew he shouldn't stare, but he couldn't quite help it.

After weeks of resisting the temptation to see her again, she'd fallen right into his lap. Metaphorically speaking, obviously. She clearly had no actual interest in his lap—or any of his other body parts. She didn't even want to admit they knew each other.

Maybe because they didn't. They'd shared one night together. What did he really know about her? Nothing. He'd learned more about her in the last half hour than he'd known when he took her to bed, a realization that didn't sit well for some reason. Especially the part about the pinot grigio.

"What's going on?" Zander muttered under his breath, dragging Ryan's attention away from the lush curve of Evangeline's hips as she bent to retrieve a bottle of red. "And don't evade the question, because something is most definitely going on here. It's written all over your face."

Ryan loved Zander like a brother, but he wasn't about to tell him the truth.

For starters, he didn't kiss and tell. What had happened between him and Evangeline was personal. She'd made it more than clear that she didn't want Zander to know they'd spent the night together, and Ryan wasn't about to out her as a liar in the middle of a job interview.

Because as uncomfortable as working together might be, she was perfect for the job.

"She's the one," he said. "Come on, can't you see it?"

Zander's eyes narrowed. "No, actually. I can't. We have at least half a dozen more qualified applicants. I'm not sure Carlo Bocci is going to be impressed by a self-proclaimed wine expert with romantic notions about tasting history in a glass of Burgundy."

"She knows her stuff. Admit it." She was smart. Ryan loved that about her. He could have sat there and listened to her talk about wine all night.

And then he would have gone home alone, obviously. Because he sure as hell couldn't go to bed with her again if she was going to work at the Bennington.

His chest grew tight at the thought. "She's a storyteller. Customers will eat that up, Bocci included."

Zander lifted a brow. "Again, why do I get the feeling there's more going on here than a simple job interview?"

Ryan didn't bother responding, but he couldn't manage to tear his gaze from Evangeline, even as Zander glared at him.

"I knew it," Zander muttered. "You're attracted to her."

"Enough," Ryan said through gritted teeth.

She was walking back toward them, cradling a bottle of Bordeaux in her hands as gently as if it were a baby.

"Just wait," he said. "Wait and see what she does with this bottle."

In actuality, Ryan wasn't sure what was about to happen. He just knew that if she didn't need a corkscrew, something interesting was sure to go down, possibly involving a butcher knife. Or maybe a hammer. He wouldn't have been surprised if she'd opened the bottle with a karate chop to its slender glass neck. Anything was possible.

"Gentlemen." She smiled and set the Bordeaux on the table. Then she swiveled her gaze back toward Elliot. "I'll need three glasses, a decanter and a small ice bucket filled with cold water."

"Of course." He gave her a little bow and disappeared to do her bidding.

She didn't even work there yet, and the staff was already treating her like she ran the place. Ryan couldn't help but smile. Even Zander was beginning to look intrigued.

Evangeline started removing items from her tote bag, one by one. First up was an old-fashioned shaving brush—the kind barbers used in the sort of establishments that had a striped pole as part of the decor. The next thing out of her bag was a small copper pot of red wax.

Just as Ryan was feeling a stab of disappointment that nothing resembling a weapon had made an appearance, she pulled out a long metal contraption with wooden handles and two arms that formed a ring where they touched.

He had no idea what he was looking at. The apparatus had sort of a medieval torture device vibe, which he supposed he shouldn't rule out as a possibility.

Beside him, Zander tilted his head. "Um..."

"Port tongs," Evangeline said. "They were invented in the eighteenth century, but these are a tad newer."

"Naturally." Ryan bit back a grin.

But it was the last item she plunked down on the table that was clearly her trump card.

It wasn't a butcher knife.

It was worse.

"Is that what I think it is?" Zander asked.

"An upright blowtorch?" She nodded. "Yes."

A look of intense alarm crossed Zander's face but before he could object, she fired it up. It made a whooshing sound, and a steady blue flame, tipped in orange, shot six or so inches into the air.

Here we go.

Elliot returned, carrying the requested items, and stopped a safe three feet away from the table. Evangeline thanked him, smiling brightly.

She's enjoying this, Ryan thought.

So was he—probably more than he should have been.

Once the items were arranged to her satisfaction, she presented the bottle of wine and described it, identifying the vintage, the vineyard and the specific area of France where it came from—the Médoc region on the Left Bank. She told them to expect a deep red liquid, with fruit scents and notes of cassis, black cherry and licorice.

Ryan had always been partial to white wine, but he had a feeling that was about to change.

Finished with her brief monologue, Evangeline set the bottle back down, picked up the port tongs and held them over the open flame until the ring burned bright red. Ryan was suddenly consciously aware of his own heartbeat and a heady combination of awe and dread pumping through his veins, as if he were on the verge of being branded.

What was happening to him? Did Zander feel it, too—this strange, sublime effect she had?

He couldn't tell, and he wasn't willing to take his eyes off her long enough to venture a glance in his cousin's direction. But he doubted it, because what he was experiencing felt an awful lot like desire.

He swallowed.

Maybe Zander was right. Maybe they'd be better off going with someone else, because having Evangeline around on a daily basis was sure to be complicated.

But that was absurd, wasn't it? He was a grown man. He could resist temptation.

Light glinted against the wine bottle in the center of the table, flashing a glimpse of the dark liquid it contained. Shimmering garnet red. Then Evangeline removed the tongs from the flame and slipped the ring over the bottle's narrow neck.

She pressed the ring in place and then loosened the tongs, rotating the ring slightly and pressing again. Satisfied, she removed the tongs altogether, placed them in a shallow pan of water and then dipped the shaving brush into the ice bucket. The bottle made a cracking sound, like ice under pressure, as Evangeline ran the brush over the spot where she'd heated the glass.

Instinct told Ryan what was coming next, but he was still thoroughly impressed when she wrapped a cloth napkin around her hand to take hold of the top of the bottle and it snapped off cleanly in her grasp.

"Voilà," she said quietly. Her bottom lip slipped between her teeth as her gaze collided with his.

Temptation.

Most definitely.

"Impressive." Zander arched a brow. "What exactly did we just witness?"

"It's called tonging," she explained as she held the little pot of red wax over the blowtorch's flame. "Traditionally, this method is reserved for opening vintage port. Aged properly, port sits for twenty, sometimes fifty years. The cork can disintegrate and crumble if you open it with a corkscrew."

She tipped the copper pot in a swirling motion until the wax ran smooth. "No one wants bits of cork in a wine they've waited half a century to drink. Tonging allows you to bypass the cork altogether."

Zander nodded. "Clever."

Evangeline dipped the severed top in the melted liquid and then did the same to the sharp edge of the bottle's remaining portion after she poured the wine into the decanter.

Crimson wax dripped down the bottle, and Ryan was struck by the fact that she'd managed to create a dramatic table decoration in addition to putting on a show.

She poured three glasses from the decanter and handed two of them to Zander and Ryan. "This is Bordeaux, not port, obviously. The method can be used to open any kind of bottle. It's rather fun, don't you think?"

Ryan sipped his wine. It was good, but try as he might, he couldn't taste cassis, black cherry and licorice. Instead, his senses swirled with the memory of their night together. He tasted Evangeline's lips, chilled from the winter air, rich with longing. He tasted her porcelain skin, sweet like vanilla.

He tasted trouble.

So very much trouble.

Zander stared into his glass. "I think—"

For the second time in the span of a half hour, Ryan cut him off. He was sure to hear about it later, but by then it would be too late. "Evangeline Holly, you're hired."

Chapter Four

She'd done it.

The job offer was conditional. After Ryan told her she was hired, Zander had added the caveat that she continue studying for her sommelier certification exam. If she didn't pass on the first try, she was out.

But that was okay, even though the test was notoriously difficult and people often had to repeat it several times. Evangeline didn't care. She'd make it work. She'd study until she knew every wine in existence.

She was a wine director! She'd gotten the job, and she'd done it all on her own.

Probably.

Maybe.

She liked to believe the tonging had secured her the position or that her knowledge and passion superseded the fact that she had no official qualifications. Or actual work experience as a sommelier, unless she counted pouring wine in the tasting room at her family's vineyard as a kid.

But that had been ages ago—nearly seventeen years. She'd been playing catch-up ever since, trying her best to put her world back together after her mother left, ripping the rug out from under her.

Ripping the rug out from under *all of them*.

Evangeline's heart gave a little tug, just like it always did when she thought about her mother, but she swallowed her feelings down. She shouldn't be dwelling on loss right now—not when she had every reason to celebrate.

"Almost every reason, anyway," she muttered.

Olive swiveled her head and gazed up at Evangeline. Bee stared straight ahead. They trotted at the ends of their leashes, tails wagging as they headed toward the dog park at the end of the block.

Their coats were dusted with snow, and tiny puffs of vapor hung in the air with every breath from the happy dogs' mouths. Despite their advanced ages, they loved going for walks. Unfortunately, the fact that they weren't supposed to be living in Evangeline's apartment meant they only got to go outside early in the morning and late at night. Thank goodness for puppy pads.

Now that she had a job—a *great* job—she needed to do something about the dog situation.

And she would.

She just wished she could shake the nagging feeling that the only reason she'd gotten the job in the first place had been because of Ryan Wilde.

He'd hired her, not Zander. And there'd been an unmistakable flash of surprise on the CEO's face when Ryan announced that the job was hers. She'd told herself to ignore it. She deserved the job. Wine was in her blood. She'd be great.

She'd simply have to avoid Ryan as much as possible. That shouldn't be too hard. He worked business hours, and Evangeline's day started at 4:00 p.m. That meant an hour or two overlap. She could survive that. Couldn't she?

Eventually, she'd be able to look at him without imagining his lips against her throat, his body rising and falling above hers. She'd be able to say his name without remembering the way she'd cried it out in the dark.

Ryan.

Ryan.

Ryan.

"It's going to be fine." She swallowed. Hard. "It's going to be fine, because it has to."

At the sound of her voice again, Olive's tail wagged even harder. Olive and Bee were the sweetest dogs in the world. She'd have kept them even if they'd been monsters, though. Even if it meant she was at risk of getting tossed out of her building.

Dogs weren't allowed at her grandfather's new extended care facility. But if Evangeline kept Olive and Bee, she could at least bring them to visit him every once in a while. She owed that much to her grandfather. Robert Holly was the one person who'd been there for her when the vineyard, and all that went with it, withered and died. The *only* one.

"You guys aren't the worst cuddle bugs to have

around," Evangeline said as they waited to cross the street. Taxis whizzed past in a dizzying blur of bright yellow against the early morning snowfall.

She glanced down at Olive, and a memory flashed instantly into Evangeline's consciousness—Ryan, shirtless, standing beside her bed, petting the little dog and looking like something out of a beefcake-bachelors-with-puppies calendar.

Oh God.

How was she supposed to work with the man every day when she couldn't stop thinking about what he looked like beneath his exquisitely tailored suit?

She'd slept with her boss. Granted, he hadn't been her boss at the time, but still. It couldn't happen again.

Obviously.

Not that Ryan had hinted at that possibility...other than a tiny wink, he'd acted purely professional during her interview. She probably should have been relieved.

Scratch that. She *was* relieved. The annoying pang in her chest wasn't disappointment. It couldn't be.

"I need to nip this situation in the bud. Right?" She clicked the double gate of the dog park closed and bent to unfasten Olive and Bee from their leashes. Olive let out an earsplitting bark—the sort of bark that would ensure their eviction if she dared to do it indoors.

Evangeline nodded. "I'll take that as a yes."

"Again?" Ryan paused in the doorway of his office and took in the sight of Zander sitting behind the desk, waiting. "Your new early hours are becoming a habit."

"Indeed they are. Get used to it." Zander shot Ryan a tight smile and waved him inside.

So this was it.

Zander had been called into a meeting immediately after their interview with Evangeline the day before, and then he'd gone home. He no longer worked late as often as he did before he married Allegra. A year ago, Ryan might have envied him.

He knew better now.

Ryan wasn't cut out for marriage...for family. He'd tried. He'd tried really hard, but it wasn't in his blood.

He'd suspected as much all along. Only a fool would grow up the way Ryan had and not wonder if a normal, healthy relationship was even in the realm of possibility. Still, when Natalie turned up pregnant, he'd allowed himself to believe.

What a mistake that had been.

A dull ache took root in Ryan's gut. He'd moved on from Natalie and her baby over a year ago. He shouldn't be thinking about that mess now—and he wouldn't be, if not for the damned *Gotham* cover hanging above Zander's head. Being heralded for his bachelor status was a pretty potent reminder that he was meant to go it alone.

"Any particular reason you're reading the morning paper in my office?" Ryan sank into one of the guest chairs. "Again?"

Zander lifted a brow. "You have to ask?"

So this *was* it.

Ryan was facing his moment of reckoning for making the unilateral decision to hire Evangeline

Holly. He should have known Zander wouldn't let it go.

"She was the right person for the job. End of story." He shrugged.

"That might be true, but as CEO I would have liked an opportunity to weigh in on the matter." Zander folded his newspaper closed and rested his elbows on the desk. "But what's done is done."

Ryan nodded. "I'm glad you see it that way."

"Are you still going to be glad when I tell you that you're going to be personally responsible for making sure Ms. Holly is a success?" Zander sat back in his chair, waiting.

Personally responsible.

What did that mean, exactly? Was Ryan supposed to hold her hand while she went table to table, recommending wines?

He'd heard worse ideas.

She's your employee now, remember?

Ryan cleared his throat. "Fine. She comes in around four. I'll plan on spending the last hour or so of each work day checking in on things upstairs."

He'd planned on keeping close tabs on Bennington 8, anyway. The chef and the rest of the staff were already aware that Carlo Bocci could turn up at any time, but Ryan wanted to ensure they were prepared. Overprepared, if possible. The Michelin ranking was too important not to oversee things personally.

"Think again," Zander said.

Something in his tone caused the ache in Ryan's gut to sharpen. "Explain, please."

Zander shrugged. Somewhere beneath his irritation, Ryan spied a hint of a smile, and he got the definite impression his cousin was enjoying playing the CEO card. "You're working nights now."

Ryan blinked.

"We'll split shifts. I'm taking days and you're handling nights. Four p.m. to midnight," Zander said.

"Whatever for?"

"So you can keep an eye on Bennington 8, obviously." Zander stood. "Someone needs to see Ms. Holly in action to make sure she's working out, and since she's your hire, that someone is you."

Ryan opened his mouth to object, then promptly closed it.

What Zander was proposing made sense on every level. Not to mention the fact that when Ryan made the decision to hire Evangeline on the spot, he'd known he'd eventually have to face the music.

And he'd done it, anyway.

Zander lingered in the doorway, arms crossed, leaning against the doorjamb. Now was the time for Ryan to fess up and tell his cousin everything.

Just say it. Do it now. Evangeline and I have a history, albeit a brief one.

He met Zander's gaze. "How long?"

"A month, probably?" Zander shrugged one shoulder. "Or until Carlo Bocci shows up. Whichever comes first."

A month, maybe even less.

Totally doable. "Sounds good."

This is about the Michelin star, he told himself. *Nothing else.*

It was work, and it had nothing whatsoever to do with Evangeline Holly. They were adults, perfectly capable of working together without falling into bed again.

Weren't they?

The closer Evangeline's footsteps got to the spinning gold door of the Bennington Hotel, the harder her heart seemed to pound in her chest. Her face was so hot she was surprised the snow flurries swirling in the air didn't sizzle and melt against her cheeks.

Was it going to be like this every day? If so, she wouldn't survive it. She'd have a heart attack right there on the rich red carpet lining the sidewalk in front of her workplace. Which might actually be convenient, because then she wouldn't have to face Ryan Wilde every day. She wouldn't have to smile politely when he held her paycheck in his hand, all the while knowing precisely where that manly hand of his had been.

One hour. She inhaled a lungful of frigid air. The immaculately dressed doorman smiled and tipped his top hat as she pushed her way through the revolving door. *Surely you can endure sixty minutes in the presence of your boss without imagining him pinning your hands over your head and kissing you against the wall.*

She swallowed.

No man had ever kissed her like that before. Like he *owned* her. She'd been shocked at how very much she'd liked it.

But she wasn't supposed to be thinking about that right now, was she? Besides, the notion that Ryan Wilde was running all over Manhattan in his Armani suit and Tiffany cuff links kissing women silly, *just like he'd kissed her,* was beyond mortifying. It actually made her sick to her stomach.

She glanced around the glittering lobby and reminded herself she was in survival mode. All she had to do was make it through the overlap in their schedules, and then she could focus. She could forget her recent lapse in judgment and concentrate on the sole area in which she excelled—wine.

It was an escape, of sorts. Tasting wine and evaluating it was almost like stopping to smell the roses. Everything around her seemed to melt away, and she lived fully in the present. It was a way of experiencing a moment in time, savoring it with every one of her senses. There was so much more to a wine than just the way it tasted. Sometimes when she swirled a particularly precious vintage in a glass, the beauty of the light shining through the liquid was so lovely, so luminous, that it almost made her weep. There were even words for that kind of clarity in a wine—brilliant, star bright.

One hour.

Then she'd be home free.

Except today it would technically be two hours, because she needed to set the record straight with her new boss, and she couldn't very well do that during her working hours. She wanted to keep her personal connection to Ryan completely separate from their working relationship—so separate that it ceased to exist.

She smiled at Elliot, the general manager who'd escorted her to the interview the day before. Her heartbeat kicked up another notch when she asked for directions to the CFO's office, but Elliot didn't bat an eye.

He motioned toward an expansive hallway and told her to turn left beneath the gleaming gold clock suspended from the lobby ceiling. "Mr. Wilde's office is second from the end, on the right-hand side. You're rather early. Can I get you anything before you head down there? Coffee or an espresso, perhaps?"

"No, thank you." She was jittery enough without adding caffeine to the mix.

Her hands were shaking, so she buried them in her pockets as she made her way across the cool marble floor. As she passed the velvet sofa where just twenty-four hours ago she'd sat waiting for her interview, she couldn't help noticing a cluster of glamorously attired women occupying the sitting area. A few of them looked familiar—so familiar that Evangeline was almost certain she recognized the brunette who'd maligned her pencil skirt.

What was going on? Were Zander and Ryan still interviewing applicants, even after offering her the job? God, she hoped not.

Relief washed over her when she reached Ryan's office and spotted him through the open door, sitting behind his desk. Alone. Not another sommelier in sight.

She took a deep breath and tapped her knuckles lightly on the open door. "Excuse me."

Ryan looked up, his crystal-blue gaze colliding with hers. Honestly, did he have to be so handsome? It was hardly fair. "Eve."

That name again. It stopped her in her tracks, and she wobbled in her stilettos.

"Evangeline," she corrected. "I don't go by Eve."

He looked at her for a beat, and she felt like she was standing in her apartment again, wrapped in bed sheets with him stretched out naked in her bed.

"Understood." He smiled, but it didn't quite reach his eyes. His gorgeous, gorgeous eyes. "Come on in."

She clicked the door closed behind her and took a seat in one of the chairs opposite his desk.

"You're early," he said before she could get a word out.

"Right." She lifted her chin. *This is it.* "I wanted to talk to you off the clock."

His gaze flitted to the windows of his corner office. Outside, the hotel's doorman stood in the center of the snowy street, waving down cabs for Bennington guests. "Shall we go elsewhere?"

"Oh." The suggestion was unexpected, but she liked the sound of it. Best to keep their personal business out of the office altogether. She nodded, but just as she was about to suggest a quick walk around Central Park, her gaze snagged on the framed picture hanging on the wall above his desk.

It was a magazine cover.

The magazine cover—the one proclaiming him bachelor of the universe or something ridiculous like that.

And he had it hanging *on the wall of his office.* "U-um," she sputtered, unable to tear her attention away from his picture on the *Gotham* cover.

Ryan followed her gaze and then stood. For once, his cool exterior seemed a little rattled. "Ah, don't pay any attention to that."

"Too late." She swallowed.

What had she been thinking? She couldn't go to the park with him. Or anywhere else, for that matter.

"It's a joke." Ryan raked a hand through his hair. "Zander thought it would be funny to hang it up in here."

"Hilarious," she said flatly.

Then he started talking about the *New York Times* and weddings and the whole thing being a big mistake, and Evangeline couldn't quite follow his rambling train of thought because something excruciatingly awful was beginning to dawn on her.

"Oh my God." Her voice echoed off the walls of Ryan Wilde's luxurious office. "*Oh my God.* Those women in the lobby—they're not here for job interviews, are they?"

"No, but..." Ryan sighed, came around his desk and took a step toward her.

Evangeline flew to her feet and pinned him with a glare. "But what? Is there or is there not a group of women just sitting in the lobby waiting for a glimpse of you, the bachelor king?"

"I'm not sure I'd put it quite that way." The corner of his mouth hitched into a self-deprecating grin.

Not that Evangeline was looking directly at his lips on purpose. It's just that he was *right there*, and his mouth was pretty much at eye level.

Still, she melted a little bit, which only magnified her embarrassment. "They thought I was one of them."

A muscle twitched in Ryan's chiseled jaw. "Pardon?"

Evangeline nodded. "Yesterday, when I was waiting for my interview, your fan club welcomed me with open arms. They even gave me some advice—lose the pencil skirt. Also, I should give up because I'm not your type."

"I'm sorry. Truly," he said.

Something in his gaze told her he was being sincere, and the room felt smaller all of a sudden. Evangeline's head spun.

He arched a brow. "As you and I both know, they're wrong."

Why was he being charming? And why was she on the verge of falling for it?

Because he's New York's hottest bachelor, you idiot.

She took a backward step, and her calves bumped into the chair where she'd been sitting. "See, this is exactly why I came here to talk to you off the clock. This—" she motioned to the space between them "—can't happen again."

He crossed his arms, but inched closer. "I absolutely agree."

She could feel his heat. Sultry and warm, like a summer's day. "I mean, you're my boss now."

His gaze dropped to her mouth. "Indeed I am."

She licked her lips. "It would be inappropriate."

"Completely." His eyes locked with hers, and she realized they were suddenly standing just a whisper apart.

The chair was no longer touching the backs of her legs. In fact, it was a good three feet away. She'd been drifting closer and closer to him the entire time, drawn to him like a moth to a flame.

She'd inched so near that she could see the fine weave of his crisp white Oxford shirt and the dark threads of the buttonhole on the wide lapel of his suit jacket. She could smell the lingering notes of his aftershave—something rich and wholly masculine. Worn leather and mossy oak with top notes of pine, sandalwood and violet leaf.

If Evangeline had known men's fragrances as thoroughly as she knew wines, she'd have been able to identify it in an instant. Alas, she didn't. But she took a deep inhale anyway, breathing him in. She felt dizzy again. Dizzy and just a little bit drunk, even though she hadn't consumed a drop of alcohol.

Stop.

Stop this right now.

If she didn't dramatically alter her course, she was going to wind up kissing him. She could already feel herself rising up on her tiptoes and tipping her face upward, toward his.

Kiss him, and you'll have no one to blame but yourself.

This was *not* the way to begin her new career. She had to do or say something to kill the mood. Immediately.

She crossed her arms—a barrier—and told what might have been the biggest lie of her life. "We'd be fools to go down that road again anyway, since last time was such a disaster."

Ryan froze for a second, then frowned. "Disaster?"

"Sure." She shrugged and feigned nonchalance as best she could. Not an easy task when every nerve ending in her body wanted to lean into him. "I'm sure you agree. It was…"

He lifted an inquisitive brow.

"...awkward." Her face went hot.

Ryan's gaze narrowed, and a mesmerizing knot flexed in his jaw. Even enraged, he was one of the most beautiful men Evangeline had ever seen.

"Awkward," he repeated without a trace of emotion in his voice.

Evangeline couldn't bring herself to look him in the eye anymore, so her gaze flitted to a blank space over his shoulder. "At best. So it obviously shouldn't happen again."

"Don't worry," he said through clenched teeth. "It won't."

"Perfect." She nodded.

He gave her a long, hard stare—one that set tiny fires skittering over her skin. Her pulse roared in her ears... *Liar, liar, liar.*

There'd been nothing awkward about that night. Nothing at all. If that had been true, she'd be capable of standing in the same room with Ryan Wilde without wanting to kiss him, without wanting his hands on her. Everywhere.

Still, it hadn't been a complete and total lie. As much as the experience had meant to Evangeline, she knew it hadn't been the same for Ryan. It just wasn't possible. She wasn't good at that sort of thing. Jeremy had made that much clear. Besides, she was pretty sure Ryan dated supermodels. Apparently, he dated *everyone.*

If she was tempted to forget that notable fact, all she had to do was glance at the magazine cover hanging on his wall.

She looked at it again, and then squared her shoulders. "I'm glad we got that settled. I know we both want what's best for Bennington 8, so it's probably a good thing we won't be working together directly."

Ryan's mouth hitched into a half grin as he resumed his place behind the desk, and the tiniest trickle of dread snaked its way down Evangeline's spine. She wasn't sure why. She'd done what she needed to do. From now on, everything should be smooth sailing.

The amused look on Ryan's face said otherwise. "I guess I should have mentioned there's been a change in plans."

A change in plans.

Why did that sound so ominous?

Ryan clasped his hands together on the surface of his desk, and a flash of silver at his wrists caught Evangeline's eye.

Cuff links.

From Tiffany & Co.

The last time she'd seen them had been six weeks ago on her nightstand.

She swallowed, and when she met his gaze again, every last trace of amusement had vanished from his expression.

He gave her a tight smile. "I'm on the night shift now, and you're working directly for me."

Chapter Five

"Hello there, stranger. Aren't you a sight for sore eyes?" Emily Wilde wrapped Ryan into a warm embrace the moment he crossed the threshold of the Wilde family brownstone.

"Hi, Emily." Ryan hugged her back, inhaling the comforting scents of Sunday dinner—of *home*—and braced himself for the inevitable tongue-lashing that was coming his way.

Emily pulled back, holding him at arm's length, but keeping a firm grip on his biceps as she pinned him with a glare. "Do you have any idea how long it's been since you showed up for weekly family dinner?"

And there it was.

"Eight weeks," she said, giving his arms a squeeze. Ryan's aunt still had the slender frame of a dancer, but she was stronger than she looked. *"Eight."*

He winced and stepped out of her grasp. "Ouch."

"You deserve worse." She swatted at him with the dishtowel in her hand. "If Zander hadn't assured me you were alive and well and helping him run that hotel of his, I would have thought you'd dropped off the face of the earth."

"I'm sorry. I've been…"

Hiding?

Licking his wounds?

Avoiding participating in family gatherings where he wasn't technically immediate family?

All of the above.

"…busy." He smiled and handed Emily the bottle of wine tucked under his arm. A peace offering.

She turned the bottle over, inspecting the label. "What's this?"

"Douro—it's a red from Portugal." He nodded toward the kitchen. "It should pair well with the lamb."

"You're not a guest here. You're family. You know that. Since when do you bring gifts to family dinner?" Emily's gaze narrowed. "Who are you, and what have you done with my son?"

My son.

A bittersweet ache burned deep in Ryan's chest. He wasn't Emily's son. Not really. But she was the closest thing to a mother he'd had for almost as long as he could remember. His memories of his birth parents were few and far between, lost in a hazy watercolor blur. They only made sense from a distance. If he focused too intently on his early years, his recollections became nothing more than shapes and colors—moody grays and blues that left him feeling empty inside.

"I'm right here." He swallowed.

"Good." His aunt nodded.

Emily Wilde was no fool. Ryan suspected she knew precisely why his presence at Sunday dinner had been scarce over the past six months or so.

He hadn't meant to pull a disappearing act. He owed everything to the family that lived in this home. But sometimes it was difficult to witness how close they all were. It almost made Ryan believe he was capable of having a family of his own someday. Which was precisely why he'd fallen so easily for Natalie's lies.

But bless her soul, Emily didn't mention Natalie. Or her baby.

"What have you got there, Mom?" Zander's gaze shot immediately to the bottle in Emily's hands when they drifted into the crowded kitchen. "Let me guess. Ryan brought it."

Every head in the room swiveled in Ryan's direction. The entire Wilde clan was there—Emily's youngest daughter, Tessa, along with her husband, Julian. Zander and Allegra. Tessa's hearing assistance dog, Mr. B, was there, too. Even Chloe, whose attendance at Sunday dinner was even more sporadic than Ryan's, was standing at the stove with a wooden spoon in her hand.

Ryan was especially glad to see Chloe. Since all the other Wilde siblings had recently coupled up, he'd become increasingly aware of his loner status. Not that it would be changing anytime soon—or ever, for that matter. He simply preferred not to dwell on it every time he walked through the brownstone's front door.

He embraced them all, one by one, then scooped Mr. B into the crook of his elbow. The little dog licked the side of his face, and his thoughts flitted briefly to the last animal he'd petted.

Evangeline's wide-eyed marshmallow of a dog.

Ryan pushed the memory back into the recesses of his mind, where it belonged, and eyed Zander over the top of Mr. B's head.

"As a matter of fact, I did bring the wine." Ryan shrugged one shoulder. "It's polite."

"It's also a wine you probably never heard of until a week ago," Zander said.

Damn.

Ryan sighed. Why had he thought the Douro had been a good idea?

Probably because you heard Evangeline waxing poetic about it last night at Bennington 8.

She'd recommended it to a large party seated at the restaurant's most prominent table. They'd been leery, but after Evangeline worked her magic with a colorful story of the vintage's history involving wine counterfeiting and at least one shipwreck, she won them over. By the end of the night, they'd consumed eight bottles.

Ryan had been intrigued.

He'd been intrigued a lot lately. Intrigued and bewildered, most notably by Evangeline's dubious assertion that their night together had been a disaster.

"I'm broadening my horizons," Ryan said blithely. "Consider it a bonus of working the night shift."

"The night shift? What's that all about?" Allegra glanced back and forth between Ryan and her husband.

Zander reached into an overhead cabinet for a

corkscrew. "Ryan's heading up our efforts to secure a Michelin star rating for Bennington 8."

Allegra's brow furrowed and her gaze flitted back to Ryan. "But you're the CFO. That seems…"

Emily finished the thought. "Odd."

Julian's hands moved rapidly, slicing the air as he summarized the conversation for Tessa in sign language. Less than five minutes had passed since Ryan walked through the door, and already the entire household was entrenched in his personal life. Marvelous.

"It's fine. I'm happy to do it," Ryan said. He didn't particularly want to get into a family-wide discussion about how his change in schedule had come about.

So he ignored the curious stares and did his best to divert attention someplace else. *Any*place else.

"The wine should breathe for an hour before it's poured." He gestured toward the bottle.

When his family continued to stand there waiting for him to elaborate on his new work schedule and his sudden interest in fermented grapes, he took the bottle of red from Zander's hands and carried it to the dining room. Blessed escape.

Away from the crowded kitchen, he could relax a bit—breathe. Especially once he heard the conversation switch gears to ballet.

It was a common topic around the brownstone. Tessa and Chloe were both professional dancers. Emily had been running the Wilde School of Dance since before Ryan was born. Nowadays, Allegra worked alongside her, teaching a majority of the classes. Even Zander had hit the dance floor for a time, competing in ballroom contests as a teen.

Ryan could fake his way through a waltz. He didn't have two left feet—he wasn't quite *that* bad—but he was no Fred Astaire. He could remember hours spent after school shuffling around the mirrored studios at the Wilde School of Dance with his arms lifted into a dance hold and a broomstick balanced across his shoulders and elbows to better his posture. He could also remember Emily wincing the numerous times his broom clattered to the floor, bringing class to an abrupt standstill. Once, he'd tripped over it and crashed into his dance partner, a pretty girl who'd gone on to win several novice competitions with a more capable companion.

Eventually, he'd begged Emily to let him quit. She'd taken mercy on him, and spending afternoons on a baseball diamond instead of the dance floor had been a relief. But being the only member of the family who hadn't contributed to the shiny collection of trophies in the dance school's lobby was another reminder that he wasn't truly one of them.

He was different.

"Thought we might need these." Zander sauntered into the dining room carrying seven red wineglasses by the bases of their stems.

Ryan relieved him of half of them and wordlessly went about placing the glasses around the table.

Zander had more on his mind than simply being helpful. Ryan could feel it. He'd worked with his cousin long enough to know when he had something he wanted to talk about. But Zander was going to have to come out and say it. Ryan didn't want to play guessing games. Especially when he couldn't even utter Evangeline's name without arousing suspicion.

"Have you seen the paper today?" Zander asked finally.

"No." Ryan shook his head.

Zander sighed. "Bocci awarded a Michelin star to one of the restaurants he reviewed this week."

"Damn. Really?"

"Really." Zander crossed his arms. "It's a little French place near Lincoln Center."

"Just one star?"

"Just one." Zander nodded. "But at the moment, that's one more star than we've got at Bennington 8."

Point taken.

The voices of the other Wildes grew louder as they drifted from the kitchen toward the dining room. Zander glanced over his shoulder and then back at Ryan. "We can talk more later, but I'd like you to go check it out and see what all the fuss is about, if you don't mind. Tomorrow night?"

Ryan shrugged. "Sure. Bennington 8 is closed tomorrow night, so the timing is perfect. But do you think I can get a reservation?"

"I already made one in your name. They're booked for weeks, but when I mentioned New York's hottest bachelor was interested, a table magically became available." Zander smiled. "See? I told you all that tabloid stuff would come in handy eventually."

Ryan rolled his eyes. "Perfect. I look forward to reading about my solo dinner in Page Six on Tuesday. They'll probably rechristen me New York's loneliest bachelor."

Zander shook his head. "You're not dining alone. The reservation is for two at nine o'clock."

"I see. We're tag teaming them, then. You're coming with?" Ryan nodded. "Probably a good idea. Dining alone might make it obvious that I'm there as a culinary spy."

"I'm glad you agree." Zander crossed his arms. His expression morphed into what Allegra jokingly called his CEO face.

Which meant that Ryan might not like what was coming next.

"Evangeline will accompany you."

Bingo.

Ryan's jaw tensed. "That's hardly a good idea."

"Why not? You said yourself that dining alone could be a problem. You've been all over the papers. If I go with you, we'll probably both be recognized and it will be obvious why we're there. If you go with Evangeline, she can check out the wine." Zander shrugged. "It'll just look like you two are on a date."

"Exactly. I'm her boss. Don't you think dating her would be a tad inappropriate?" Ryan fixed his gaze on the table and straightened a wineglass that didn't need straightening.

Could he be a bigger hypocrite right now?

Granted, he hadn't slept with her while she'd been employed at the Bennington. In fact, they'd barely exchanged more than two words since their "off-the-record" discussion in his office on her first day. They'd been tiptoeing around one another every night, avoiding eye contact.

But there'd been one or two times he'd caught her staring when she thought he wasn't looking. And the way her cheeks went pink and her lips parted when she'd been caught told him she'd been lying through her teeth about their night together.

A disaster?

Hardly.

Zander snorted. "Of course I think dating her would be inappropriate. It would be worse than that, actually. It would be a disaster."

That word again—*disaster*.

Ryan's head snapped up. "I'm not sure I'd go that far."

"I would. We can't afford that kind of distraction while Bocci is in town. Besides, aren't you forgetting something? Tomorrow won't actually *be* a date," Zander said.

Right. Ryan had indeed forgotten that significant detail.

Zander frowned. "I'm not asking you to date her. In fact, I'm specifically asking you *not* to. I don't even want you pretending to date her. I'm just saying if people see you dining together and jump to the wrong conclusion, so be it. Why are you fighting me on this?"

Because date or not, he couldn't sit across from her without thinking about her blue eyes glittering in the darkness, her kittenish sighs and the way her breath caught in her throat when he pushed inside her.

Something in his chest tightened and closed like a fist. "It's fine. I'll do it."

Zander cut Ryan a glance as the rest of the family spilled into the room, piling plates onto the table. "Good. That was the answer I expected five minutes ago."

"Tell me about your new job." Robert Holly, Evangeline's grandfather, sat in his beige leather recliner with Olive and Bee piled in his lap.

If Evangeline tried really hard, she could almost pretend they were back in his old apartment on Forty-Second Street instead of a nursing home she could barely afford. But no amount of pretending could dislodge the lump from her throat. As grateful as she was that he'd been able to bring a few pieces of furniture from home and the staff allowed her to bring the dogs by to visit once a week, she still wished things could be different.

He was putting on a brave face, but the nurses had already told Evangeline he'd seemed depressed since he'd moved in. Somehow, the fact that he was protecting her feelings instead of the other way around only made her feel worse.

But that's how it had always been. Grandpa Bob was more than just a grandfather. He was her family—what was left of it, anyway. Old habits died hard.

"My job?" Where to start? *Let's see—with my famous bachelor boss who I accidentally slept with or the fact that the late-night hours are killing me?*

She'd fallen asleep standing straight up in the wine cooler the night before. When she'd woken up, she'd spied Ryan watching her from across the room, his dark gaze as penetrating as ever through the frosted glass. Or maybe she'd just been dreaming of him. She hadn't quite decided which prospect was more mortifying.

"The job is fine." She smiled, then blinked in an effort to eradicate the image of Ryan Wilde in one of his sleek designer suits from her mind. Hopeless.

"Fine?" Grandpa Bob's hand paused, midscratch, on the top of Bee's furry little head. "You thought you wouldn't be able to land a sommelier position until you passed your certification exam. I assumed the reason you've been glowing since you walked in here was because you'd snagged your dream job."

"It is. I have." Her face went hot. "I mean, I'm not glowing."

"You are," he countered.

"I'm not." Evangeline's gaze narrowed. "You're not wearing your glasses. I probably just look blurry around the edges."

That had to be it, because she was absolutely not *glowing* when she thought about Ryan Wilde. He had enough women glowing all over Manhattan.

Her grandfather laughed, and her face grew even warmer.

She cleared her throat. "It's definitely my dream job. It's just a tad more challenging than I thought it would be."

She would have liked to blame Ryan, just because. But while she might have been able to convince herself that his mere presence was distracting to the point of exhaustion, it didn't explain why she'd been unable to accurately identify any of the whites at her wine study group earlier this afternoon.

She was off her game.

That never happened.

Evangeline was the best taster in the group. Usually, anyway. When she'd confidently classified the second glass in the tasting as a sauvignon blanc from the southern Bordeaux region of France, the other members of the group had simply stared at her with their mouths agape.

Now wasn't the time to be making those kinds

of mistakes. Not when there was a Michelin star on the line.

"I'll be fine, though. I was born for that job." Again, she was distracted. That was all.

Had she been rattled by Ryan's announcement that he was changing to the night shift and she was to work directly under him? Sure. But she'd survived the first week, hadn't she?

Survived *might be a stretch. You've been hiding from him for five straight days.*

"Of course you were born for it." Grandpa Bob nodded. His smile quickly faded and was replaced with a pensive expression that made her heart feel like it was being squeezed in a vise. "I'm only sorry I couldn't save the vineyard. I didn't know..."

Evangeline shook her head in an effort to get him to stop.

She couldn't believe he'd brought up the vineyard. They'd spent almost two decades steadfastly avoiding the topic. It hurt too much to think about so much loss, and besides, he'd done nothing wrong. Not one thing.

Losing the vineyard had been her father's doing. And in a way, her mother's.

"It's okay. The job at the Bennington is the chance I've been waiting for. It's a fresh start." And boy, did she ever need one. For once she was glad that her grandfather never seemed to remember Jeremy's name. At least she wouldn't have to explain the breakup. And the subsequent job loss.

She wasn't exactly lying to Grandpa Bob. She was protecting him from the ugly truth. His whole life had recently been turned upside-down. All he needed to know was that she'd gotten a new job working as a sommelier at one of the most exclusive hotels in New York.

For now.

She pasted on a smile and ignored the churning in the pit of her stomach. She could be the best damn sommelier the Bennington could hope for. Better, even. She simply needed to get some rest, clear her head and most of all, rid her thoughts of Ryan Wilde.

That's what days off were for, right?

She nodded resolutely, and then, as if fate itself were mocking her, her cell phone chimed with an incoming text. She glanced at the display as Grandpa Bob switched gears and began talking about pizza night in the nursing home's dining room.

Zander Wilde: Sorry to bother you on your day off, but are you available to evaluate a restaurant tonight?

She stared at the words on the tiny screen. Before she could type a response, the phone chimed again.

Zander Wilde: Should have mentioned it's a Michelin-starred restaurant. Would like your input on the wine.

Here it was…her chance to get back on track and prove her worth without being distracted by Ryan's handsome face popping into her periphery every five minutes.

She really needed to stop thinking about how good-looking he was.

And she would.

Starting right now.

"Sorry, Grandpa. I just need to answer this text. It looks like I'll have to work tonight after all."

"Go right ahead. Do what you need to do, although we'll miss you around here this evening at pizza night." He smiled. Olive and Bee peered up at her, wagging their tails.

Pizza with a bunch of senior citizens and two snuggly dogs actually sounded lovely, but so did dinner at an upscale eatery that had been awarded a coveted Michelin star. Especially if she could enjoy said dinner with the very professional, very married Zander Wilde instead of his hot bachelor of a cousin.

She tapped out a response.

Evangeline Holly: Of course. Where and when should I meet you?

Zander Wilde: The Bennington limo will pick you up at 8.

Perfect.

Chapter Six

"We're here, sir." Tony, the Bennington chauffeur, met Ryan's gaze in the rearview mirror of the limousine. "Shall I go fetch Ms. Holly?"

Ryan glanced at the steps leading up to Evangeline's building and the intricately carved red door that, seven weeks ago, had been shut so resolutely in his face. "No, I'll do it."

He had no idea what Zander had told her about this impromptu field trip. When he'd mentioned calling Evangeline to discuss arrangements for transportation, Zander assured him it was already taken care of.

Surely he'd warned her that Ryan would be her companion for the four-course meal awaiting them at Mon Ami Jules on the Upper West Side. Then again, why would Zander consider Ryan's presence worth mentioning? As he'd reiterated more than once, this wasn't a date. It was business.

All the same, he doubted she'd be thrilled to find him waiting for her in the intimate confines of the limo's back seat unless she was expecting him. She might even consider it *disastrous*. If she was going to toss that word out again, Ryan preferred it to happen outside of Tony's earshot.

"Yes, sir," Tony said with a nod. "I'll wait at the curb."

Ryan climbed out of the sleek black car. Rock salt crunched beneath his feet as he made his way up the steps, and a sensation that felt too much like desire stirred deep in his gut as he approached Evangeline Holly's threshold.

It's not a date—pretend, real or otherwise.

His jaw clenched, and he rapped on the door.

The knock was met with an explosion of barks coming from within the apartment. The door swung open at once, revealing a panicked Evangeline stooping to shush the two little spaniels that Ryan had encountered on his previous visit.

"Olive and Bee," he said. The pendulum swing of their tails intensified at the sound of their names. "Nice to see you again."

Evangeline popped up, ramrod straight, with a dog tucked beneath each arm. They both squirmed gleefully as the color drained from Evangeline's exquisite face. Her perfect pink mouth fell open, and Ryan's gaze flitted briefly to her tongue.

A thousand inappropriate ideas came to mind. Possibly more.

Each and every one of them began with capturing her face in his hands and holding her still while he kissed her again. Slowly...deeply.

Thoroughly.

"You," she finally said, without any sort of preamble.

He'd been right. Zander clearly hadn't been forthcoming with the details. Score one for intuition.

"Expecting someone else?" Ryan arched a brow.

She shook her head. Too hard. Too fast. "No."

Ryan arched his brow a notch higher.

She sighed. "Okay, yes. I might have thought I was meeting Zander for dinner."

He shrugged one shoulder as he reached to give Olive a scratch behind one of her copper-colored ears, remembering to approach her from the left side since she was blind in her right eye. "Sorry to disappoint."

"I'm not disappointed," she said without meeting his gaze. "Just..."

"Rattled?"

The last time they'd been alone together, they'd nearly ended up in a lip-lock, despite vowing to one another it was a terrible idea. He knew she was rattled. Hell, so was he.

Her cheeks flared pink.

"No. Surprised, that's all," she countered.

"Good, because there's no reason to be nervous around me, Evangeline. None. I'm certainly not going to force myself on you." His attention drifted to her mouth again. Damn it. "Nor am I going to kiss you."

She swallowed hard, and he traced the movement up and down the slender column of her throat before forcing himself to look her in the eye. "You have my word. This is a business dinner."

For a long, loaded moment, neither of them said anything. Evangeline's eyes glittered like frosted blue diamonds, but somewhere in their luminous depths, Ryan could have sworn he saw a spark of disappointment. Or maybe that was just wishful thinking on his part.

"A business dinner." Evangeline nodded. "Of course. What else would it be?"

She shot him a bright smile. So bright that he knew it wasn't real.

What were they doing? This was absurd. They were obviously attracted to each other. Would it really be so bad to act on that attraction...again?

"Eve..." He knew he wasn't supposed to call her that, but it was a deliberate choice. It was easier to pretend at the Bennington, to deny the pull he felt toward her. The need.

But they weren't at the Bennington now. Here, they'd touched. Here, they'd kissed. They'd been different people here. It was impossible to pretend otherwise.

She took a deep breath, and he could see the struggle in her eyes. He could feel it in the way her body arched toward him, as if they were dance partners.

Then one of the dogs emitted a snuffling sound somewhere between a bark and sneeze, and the magic spell was broken. Ryan heard footsteps behind him. Evangeline's gaze shot over his shoulder, and faster than he could process, she shoved Olive at his chest, grabbed his wrist and hauled him inside her apartment.

The door slammed shut.

Ryan stumbled backward. "What the...?" Olive

licked his left eye before he could complete the thought.

He squeezed his eyes closed, and when he opened them, he found Evangeline peering through the peephole, clutching Bee. Her hand was clasped gently over the dog's mouth.

They were hiding, apparently. Ryan just wasn't sure why. Or from whom.

He watched, waiting, until she spun around.

"Good girl," she whispered, and set Bee down on the floor.

The little Cavalier immediately began pawing at Ryan's shins. He glanced at the dog, then back up at Evangeline. Her cheeks went crimson.

His eyes narrowed. "Care to let me in on your little secret?"

She crossed her arms, then promptly uncrossed them. In the light of her apartment, he got a better glimpse at what she was wearing beneath her blush-colored coat—a dress with a feathered skirt and a bit of sparkle on the bodice. She looked more elegant than he'd ever seen her before. Elegant, and fully embarrassed.

She bit her lip. Ryan had to force himself not to focus on her mouth again. "Olive and Bee might not technically be allowed to live here."

He glanced down at the dog nestled in the crook of his elbow and then at the other one—Bee— who flopped onto her back at his feet, begging for a belly rub. Sweet dogs. No doubt about it. High-maintenance, though. Not exactly the types of pets that could go unnoticed. They weren't goldfish, for crying out loud.

He set Olive down on the floor beside Bee and, as if to confirm his thoughts on the matter, they immediately began chasing one another in a loop around Evangeline's flowery, Shabby Chic sofa.

"I'm guessing that was one of your neighbors outside just now?" Ryan said.

She nodded.

He let out a laugh. "Good luck keeping them a secret. You're going to need it."

She sighed. "It's not funny."

"Actually, it is. A little bit, anyway." One of the dogs barked, and Ryan shrugged. "I rest my case."

"Bee is deaf. Her bark is loud because she's trying to hear herself."

Understandable, but somehow Ryan didn't think her landlord would care about that sad little tidbit. "You have one dog that can't see and another that can't hear?"

"Yes," she said, as if it were completely normal. "Bee is Olive's seeing eye dog. Olive is Bee's ears. They help each other."

It was official. He was in a Hallmark movie.

Evangeline brushed past him, toward the kitchen. He had a vague, wine-drenched memory of kissing her there—Evangeline sitting on the counter, her lithe arms draped around his neck. He blew out a steadying breath and averted his gaze. There was a slender wine cabinet in the living room—empty, save for a lone bottle of red.

She returned with two rawhide bones, one for each dog. They immediately settled onto opposite ends of the couch with their treasures.

Evangeline turned toward him, and a self-satisfied

smirk tipped her lips. "See? Easy-peasy. No one will know they're here."

"For the next five minutes maybe. Although I must say, I admire your ability to convince yourself otherwise. It takes a special kind of optimism to so willingly deny the truth." He shot her a pointed look.

They weren't talking about the dogs anymore, and they both knew it.

That ridiculous word—*disaster*—floated between them. Such a blatant lie.

Evangeline's gaze flitted around the room. She seemed to be focusing on anything and everything other than him. "Were you telling the truth earlier when you promised not to kiss me?"

"Yes." Somewhere in the back of his head, a voice told him not to make promises he couldn't keep. He paused and reconsidered. "With one exception."

She licked her lips, an unconscious gesture that would have no doubt rattled her if she'd been aware of it. "And what might that be?"

He waited for her to look at him before he answered. "If you ask me to. Nicely, of course."

It was the only way.

He was her boss, and he didn't want to take advantage of her. But if she wanted him badly enough to ask him to kiss her, to touch her, he'd never be able to deny her. Wild horses wouldn't be able to stop him.

Her blue eyes flashed. "Now who's delusional? You think I'm going to beg you to kiss me?"

"I never said beg. That was your choice of words." He couldn't suppress his smile any longer. He grinned at her, full wattage. "Although the prospect does have a certain appeal."

"If you want someone to beg, there are probably half a dozen women in the Bennington lobby right now who I'm sure would be more than willing to oblige," she said tartly.

Touché.

He took a step closer—close enough that he could see her pulse pounding in the hollow of her throat. "If you want me to kiss you, you're going to have to ask."

"Understood, but just so we're clear—that's never going to happen." Her voice was a ragged whisper, with a hint of vulnerability that crushed something tender and raw deep in his chest.

He had to pause for a moment before he responded.

"Fine. We should probably get going, anyway. There's a car waiting outside, and our reservations are in less than fifteen minutes." He steadied the un-characteristic tremble in his hands by busying himself with buttoning his coat. "But you know what they say."

"What's that?" she asked warily.

"Never say *never*."

The ride uptown through the snowy city streets was excruciating. Who knew it was possible to be so thoroughly miserable while sitting in the back seat of a luxury limousine?

Or quite so…restless.

Evangeline squirmed against the buttery soft leather at her back and did her best to ignore Ryan's presence beside her. But no matter how hard she fo-cused on the delicate snowflakes melting against the car's darkened windows, she could still feel the warmth of his body, so close to hers. She still shuddered when her thigh brushed against the smooth wool fabric of his bespoke suit pants.

If you want me to kiss you, you're going to have to ask.

She couldn't get those words out of her head. They twirled round and round—irresistibly sweet, like spun sugar.

Worst of all, he knew she couldn't stop thinking about them. She was certain of it. Every time she snuck a sideways glance at him, the corner of his mouth tugged into a sly grin. It was beyond embarrassing.

She wouldn't ask him to kiss her, obviously. His enticing little ultimatum might have planted the idea right at the forefront of her thoughts, but she'd never act on it. He'd lost his mind if he thought she would. Such reverse psychology might work on the hordes of bachelorettes who threw themselves in his path, but not Evangeline.

Then why are you still thinking about it?

She glared at Ryan.

He regarded her with those blue eyes that always seemed to see too much. "Something on your mind, Miss Holly?"

The man was impossible.

"Yes," she said primly. "Where are we going? Zander didn't mention the name of the restaurant."

Among other things.

The next time Zander requested her presence somewhere, she was going to make sure to get the details. She still couldn't believe she'd unknowingly walked right into this situation.

"It's a little French place near Lincoln Center. Mon

Ami something or other." Ryan's French accent was perfect, because of course it was.

But Evangeline didn't particularly care about his impressive language skills. A horrible sense of dread had washed over her, and she could barely force her next words out. *"Mon Ami Jules?"*

It couldn't be. *No.* Please, *no.*

"That sounds right." He angled his head toward her. "You know it?"

She knew it, all right. Mon Ami Jules was the restaurant where she was supposed to be employed— *Jeremy's* restaurant.

She couldn't have dinner there. Absolutely not. She'd rather cook dinner for Ryan herself.

Not that cooking him dinner would be in any way relevant to the Bennington or Carlo Bocci.

She was losing it. She was one hundred percent losing her mind. "I've heard of Mon Ami Jules. Honestly…"

Honestly? She had no intention of being truthful. She was planning on trying to diplomatically extricate herself from the situation by saying she already knew everything there was to know about Mon Ami Jules. But before she could say another word, the limo slowed to a stop in front of Jeremy's bistro.

Her mouth grew dry as she stared out the window at the fresh Michelin star insignia placed prominently on the building's glossy front door. She couldn't believe what she was seeing. The Michelin star hadn't even been on Jeremy's radar. Before their breakup, he'd simply been focused on getting his kitchen up and running—oh, and sleeping with his sous chef in his spare time. Who had the hours to pursue excellence when there was so much sex to be had?

And now the Michelin star had fallen into his lap. The unfairness of it churned in Evangeline's stomach, twisting into a sickening knot.

She'd been the focused one. She'd been the one who'd played by the rules. Always.

Almost always… She'd made one notable mistake, and he happened to be sitting beside her at the moment, clearly baffled as to why she couldn't seem to get out of the car.

Tony held the car door open for her, but she remained rooted to the spot, unable to move.

"Now's the part where we go inside and have dinner." Ryan straightened the already-perfect Windsor knot in his tie and nodded toward the dark green awning where *Mon Ami Jules* was spelled out in elegant script.

The tangle of dread in her stomach tightened, and bile rose to the back of her throat.

Oh God.

She was going to have to do it, wasn't she? She was going to have to walk in there and pretend she was having the time of her life while she shared a lengthy four-course dinner with Ryan Wilde in her ex's restaurant.

"Evangeline," Ryan prompted, his expression growing more serious. Wary even, as if he was afraid she might do something crazy like refuse to emerge from the back seat.

No way. She wouldn't give him the satisfaction of thinking he'd rattled her to such an extent that she couldn't do something as simple as sit across a table from him and eat a dish of beef bourguignonne. Nor would she jeopardize her job and hide from Jeremy when she'd done nothing wrong. *He* was the cheater. She had nothing to be ashamed of.

Still, her legs wobbled beneath her as she climbed out of the limousine. She was actually grateful for the gentle pressure of Ryan's palm on the small of her back, steadying her, as his touch seemed to smolder right through the beaded bodice of her dress.

"Wilde, party of two," he said to the hostess.

"Yes, of course." She fluttered her eyelashes at him without giving Evangeline so much as a cursory glance.

So this is what it must feel like to go on a date with the city's most eligible bachelor.

Oh joy.

They were quickly seated at a table for two in the far corner of the crowded dining room. At least six tables had been added since the last time Evangeline had stood in the cozy, wood-paneled space. Every one of them was full at the moment. She glanced around and didn't set eyes on a single unoccupied chair.

"I guess a Michelin star really does translate into a full reservation book," she muttered once she and Ryan were alone, menus in hand.

"Exactly." He reached for the wine list and slid it across the crisp, white tablecloth toward Evangeline. "Give it a look. See what you think."

She scanned the selection. Six reds, seven whites plus a generous offering of champagnes, ranging from extra brut to doux. All French. "It's a finely tuned list, but appropriate given the dinner menu."

Ryan frowned. "How can you know that? You haven't opened your menu yet."

Busted.

She blinked. "It's a French bistro, with a French name. I'm assuming all the cuisine is French, as well."

She really didn't want to get into the sad, sordid history of her love life. Not here. And definitely *not* with Ryan.

Was it too much to hope that Jeremy would stay in the kitchen all evening and she'd never be forced to look him in the face or, heaven forbid, introduce him to her bachelor boss?

God, she hoped not.

"Well, I hope you like foie gras because the cuisine here seems pretty one-note," Ryan said drily.

She pulled a face. "I don't, actually. Do you know how foie gras is made? It's inhumane and just plain mean."

"That makes sense coming from a woman presently risking eviction for the sake of two special-needs dogs." He closed his menu and pushed it aside. "What's the story there, anyway?"

Why did he care?

She swallowed. "I thought we established this is a business dinner."

"It is, but that doesn't mean we can't have a conversation about something other than the Bennington. It's going to be a long night if we sit here in silence, don't you think?"

He had a point.

She took a deep breath. *It's not a date.* "I think I told you that until recently Olive and Bee belonged to my grandfather. He can't have pets where he is now, so I took them in."

Ryan studied her in that way he had that always made her heart beat too hard. Too fast. "Even though you live in a building that doesn't allow animals?"

"I didn't have a choice," she said.

"Yes, you did. But not many people would choose what you did."

She rolled her eyes. "Why? Because I'm an idiot?"

"On the contrary. It means you're caring. Passionate." The still, silent way he held her gaze made her head spin a little.

It was a relief when the sommelier interrupted their conversation to take the wine order. Evangeline tore her gaze away from Ryan to consider the gentleman standing over them, holding a corkscrew. Her replacement, presumably. Her heart sank a little when she spotted the lapel pin on the man's suit jacket, indicating he'd already passed the advanced sommelier exam.

Without missing a beat, Ryan declined to choose a wine and instead asked the sommelier for a recommendation. A test. He suggested a Côtes du Rhône, an uninspired choice, as far as Evangeline was concerned. But what did she know?

She was beginning to get the definite feeling she was in over her head. Being back on Jeremy's turf was getting to her. He'd replaced her, in every way possible.

"Well?" Ryan asked after the sommelier had gone. "What do you think?"

"I think you're wrong. I'm far from passionate.

That seems to be the consensus, anyway." The words flew right out of her before she could stop them.

She didn't know what it was about Ryan that made her say things she ordinarily wouldn't dream of saying.

Ryan went still. "I was referring to the wine selection."

"Right. Of course you were. Um, the wine sounds fine." She clamped her mouth closed before she said something else even more humiliating. Although she was hard-pressed to think of anything more embarrassing than announcing she was deficient in the passion department.

"Fine? The wine is *fine*? I know that can't be right." He furrowed his brow, oh-so-handsomely.

She really didn't have the energy to argue with him. It was all she could do just to get through this horrible night. "It's a Côtes du Rhône. I'm sure it will be lovely."

"I've never heard you describe a wine in so few words before." Clearly he had no intention of letting it go. "The Evangeline Holly that I know tends to wax poetic about such matters."

She busied herself with meticulously unfolding and refolding the napkin in her lap so she wouldn't have to look him in the eye...

...until he said the words that made her heart stop. "Which is just one of the reasons that I know she's brimming with passion."

Her gaze collided with his, and the way he was looking at her left no doubt he was telling the truth.

"Shall I list the other reasons? Or would that be

inappropriate, given this is a business dinner? Your call." His deep voice rolled over her in a wave.

She sat stone still. She didn't trust herself to breathe, much less speak.

He was saying everything she'd once longed to hear from Jeremy. And for reasons she couldn't fathom, those words meant even more coming from Ryan. Somewhere along the way, his opinion had become the one that mattered. She wasn't sure when, or how, but it had.

"Seriously, Evangeline. Whoever told you that you lack passion is a fool." He leaned forward, looming above the candle in the center of the table, eyes blazing.

"It's there. I've seen it. I've felt it. I've *tasted* it. If you're wondering if I'm talking about the night we spent together, the answer is yes. But it's not just that. It's more. So much more. It's the way you sliced the top off that champagne bottle and the history lessons you give everyone before you'll let them taste a sip of wine. It's the way your eyes go all soft when you talk about your grandfather, and yes, it's the way your breath catches in your throat when you and I are in the same room together. It's the way you're looking at me right now. I go to bed every night—alone, contrary to what you might think—and I dream about that look. That's passion, Evangeline. And you're no stranger to it."

He stopped abruptly, sighing mightily as the sommelier returned.

Neither of them said a word while he presented the wine for Ryan's inspection, then uncorked the bottle. An agonizing lump swelled in Evangeline's throat. She felt like crying all of a sudden, and she wasn't sure why.

She did her best to focus on the swirl of dark liquid in her wineglass as the sommelier poured, but her gaze was drawn back to Ryan's like a magnet. And when their eyes met once again, she saw her own yearning written all over his face.

The sommelier lingered, waiting.

Evangeline had zero interest in the wine. None. She reached for her glass but stopped short of taking hold of it. There was a visible tremor in her fingertips as she rested her hand on the tablecloth.

Ryan sipped from his glass and nodded. "Very good, thank you."

At last the sommelier left.

Evangeline took a deep breath. Words were bubbling up her throat—words she'd been trying her best not to say since the moment she'd woken up beside Ryan Wilde. There was no stopping them now. Not anymore. Not after what he'd just told her.

"Ryan, I…"

From somewhere behind her, a voice interrupted. "Evangeline?"

And just like that, the warm glow rising up from deep inside her soul vanished.

She didn't turn around. She didn't have to.

Jeremy.

Chapter Seven

Another interruption.

Ryan's jaw tensed to the point of pain. He dragged his gaze away from Evangeline to get a look at the man who'd just said her name. It was the chef, if the toque on the man's head was any indication.

And yet not *just* the chef, Ryan realized as he watched the color drain from Evangeline's face.

"Hello, Jeremy," she said quietly.

The chef—Jeremy, apparently—shot a curious glance at Ryan, then turned back to Evangeline. "I didn't know you had a reservation. Did you come here to see me?"

Ryan had the sudden overwhelming urge to hit something. Or someone. At the moment, the chef seemed like a good target. Who exactly was this guy?

Jealous much?

He took a strained inhale. He had no claim on Evangeline and therefore, no right to feel this way. Somehow knowing that didn't help matters.

Ryan's own words from moments ago rang like a bell in his consciousness.

Seriously, Evangeline. Whoever told you that you lack passion is a fool.

"I'm here for dinner." Evangeline lifted her chin and leveled her gaze at Jeremy, undoubtedly the fool in question.

Her body language gave her away—the crossed arms, the fixed stare, the rebellious tilt of her head. But beyond the bravado, he saw the way her sapphire eyes seemed to go bluer than he'd ever seen before.

Jeremy had hurt her. The pain was real. Raw. Fresh.

"Excellent. I hope you enjoy yourselves." Jeremy glanced at Ryan again.

Evangeline's gaze flitted back and forth between the two men. "Ryan, this is Jeremy, the chef here at Mon Ami Jules. Jeremy, this is…"

An awkward pause followed, as if she wasn't sure how to introduce him. Ryan tried to imagine her possible options. Her boss? The one-night stand she probably regretted?

Neither of those was bearable.

"Ryan Wilde." He stood and offered his hand.

The chef took it and gave it a shake. "Jeremy Peters."

Ryan complimented the menu, and they exchanged a few words about French cuisine. Small talk. Ryan couldn't concentrate on any of it. He was too preoccupied with the dull ache that had formed at the base of his skull. He didn't want to be here in this man's restaurant, eating his food and shaking his hand while the tenuous connection he'd just made with Evangeline broke beneath the strain.

They'd had a moment, and it was fading away as surely as a pink-hued sky after a blazing sunset.

He sat back down, hoping Jeremy Peters would take the hint and go away. Instead, he droned on and on, oblivious to the way Evangeline blanched after her first sip of wine. She was so obviously disgusted by it that Ryan had to stifle a grin. Their eyes met, and her lips quivered with mirth when he reached for his glass. It tasted fine to him. Quite good, actually. But what did he know? After all, he still indulged in the occasional glass of pinot grigio.

He took another swallow, then a few more. Evangeline's eyes widened ever so slightly in amused horror. Again, Jeremy seemed clueless to what was transpiring at the table. He continued his monologue with a meticulously detailed description of his coq au vin.

They were sharing a secret right beneath his nose, and the connection between them—that glittering, gossamer thread—dazzled brightly once again, warming Ryan from the inside out.

He took another gulp of the Côtes du Rhône and then set his wineglass back down on the table, toying with the stem as memories he'd been doing his best to push away came rushing into his consciousness. Denying them was a hopeless effort. In recent weeks, he'd been semisuccessful in forcing his mind into submission whenever it strayed toward forbidden territory. But it was no use...there was no forgetting.

The memories weren't just in his head. They lived in his body—in his shuddering breath, in the featherlight nerve endings on his lips and the tips of his fingers. His flesh remembered her. It remembered every caress, every whispered sigh, every exquisite thing about that night.

He looked at her, sitting across from him in her glittering, feathered dress, and despite the suddenly awkward circumstances, she seemed to glow. God, she was gorgeous. Focusing so intently on her luminous eyes and lush, kissable lips was far too dangerous, so he dropped his gaze to her delicate hand resting on the table, just out of reach.

And yet so close…so very close…

Desire rippled through him, blossoming from somewhere deep inside, drawing him toward her. It was a fierce, fiery thing, visible in the uncontrollable tremor in his fingertips as his hands inched slowly toward hers.

He could have stopped himself. He could have simply withdrawn his hand and curled it into a fist under the table, but he didn't want to. Not after the way she'd looked at him as he'd confronted her with evidence of her passion. Not while a sly smile tipped her lips. Secret. Special. Only for him.

He slid his hand forward until the tips of his fingers made contact with hers. It was the barest of touches, little more than nothing. But somehow, some way, *everything*.

Evangeline let out a little gasp, and her gaze fluttered toward his. He waited a beat, and when she didn't pull away, he fully took her hand, weaving her slender fingers through his until he wasn't sure where his touch ended and hers began.

Ryan couldn't remember the last time he'd held hands with a woman.

College, maybe? As far back as high school?

PDA had never been his thing, but there was something different about Evangeline. If they'd been lovers—*real* lovers, not simply two people who'd once been intimate—he'd never be able to keep his hands off her.

But they weren't. Perhaps that was why there was a hint of melancholy in the warmth of their touch, and perhaps that was why the simple act of holding her hand felt more meaningful than he could ever have imagined. Perhaps that was why he couldn't seem to let go.

Jeremy looked down, spotted their interlaced fingers and at last grew quiet.

He cleared his throat. "Well, I've kept you long enough. Enjoy your dinner. Don't worry about ordering. I'll send over the chef's special tasting menu. It's on the house."

Ryan and Evangeline thanked him, and at long last, he was gone.

Their eyes met, and Evangeline's cheeks flared pink. She gave him a smile so soft, so vulnerable, that he forgot all the reasons he shouldn't be sitting across from her on a glittering Manhattan evening, holding her hand.

"Thank you," she said.

"For what, exactly?"

Her eyes flitted briefly in the direction where Jeremy had gone. The kitchen, presumably. "For making an awkward situation more bearable."

The sommelier returned to refill Ryan's glass, and Evangeline grew quiet. Ryan nodded his thanks, and was forced to release Evangeline's hand in order to accommodate the sommelier.

"Am I correct in assuming that Jeremy is an ex?" he asked once they were alone again.

"Yes. It ended badly." She nodded, and once again, a flash of pain glimmered in her eyes.

Ryan's gut tightened. Then he asked a question to which he somehow already knew the answer. "When?"

She stiffened ever so slightly, then shrugged an elegant, bare shoulder. "A while ago."

"A while." He took another, larger, taste of his wine. "As in six or seven weeks?"

"Thereabouts." She reached for her own glass, brought it to her lips, then frowned into it and placed it back on the table.

"Ah." He nodded.

Six or seven weeks ago, which meant the breakup occurred shortly before they'd met one another. The night he'd gone home with her.

Suddenly that evening made much more sense, as did Evangeline's skittishness the following morning. He'd wanted to see her again. *Needed* to. But there'd been no convincing her. Now he knew why.

He stared at the swirl of burgundy liquid in his glass, suddenly wishing it were something stronger. The timing shouldn't have mattered. He knew it shouldn't, but somehow it did. He wasn't even sure why.

Yes, you are.

The timing mattered because everything about that night mattered. It had mattered to him, anyway. And he was pretty damn sure it mattered to her, too.

"*Oeuf cocotte à la parisienne.* Parisian shirred egg, compliments of the chef." A server placed a small blue crock in the center of the table.

Ryan took an exploratory bite and was somewhat disappointed to discover the dish was delicious. "Not bad."

Evangeline didn't offer an opinion. Dishes kept coming, one after another. There was no more time for conversation, no opportunity to slip back into the quiet intimacy they'd fallen into before. Ryan was glad when the meal finally came to an end.

They sat side by side in the back of the limo as it crawled through the snowy streets, Manhattan nothing more than a silvery, sparkling blur through the frosted windows. The inside of the car was snug and warm, and once again, their fingertips came to rest a fraction of an inch apart on the smooth leather seat between them.

So close. And still so maddeningly far away.

The driver's voice crackled through the car's intercom system sooner than seemed possible. "We've arrived at Miss Holly's building."

Ryan pushed the button on his side of the partition. "Thank you, Tony. I'll escort Miss Holly to her door."

If it had been a day earlier, he'd have expected her to protest and insist that Tony walk her up the front steps of her building instead. Something had changed tonight, though. It felt as if he knew her now. *Really* knew her.

All that nonsense about their night together being a disaster?

She actually believed it, just not in the way he'd originally thought. Evangeline was convinced she'd been a disappointment, which couldn't have been further from the truth. It made him want to strangle that pompous foodie ex of hers...

Right after he took her to bed again and showed her exactly how much passion she kept hidden away in that beautifully guarded exterior of hers. But that wasn't going to happen. Not tonight, anyway. For a multitude of reasons, most of which had nothing whatsoever to do with Bennington 8.

He climbed out of the back seat and rounded the car, bowing his head against the winter wind, and then opened her door. "After you."

She stepped out and slipped past him, leaving a trace of airy floral scent behind her. Wholly feminine and just a little bit wild, like sun-kissed orchids.

Ryan took a deep breath and pressed his hand on to the small of her back as they navigated the icy sidewalk. Evangeline's neighborhood was dark. Quiet. Serenely so. The hum of the limo idling at the curb was the only sound piercing the silence. Ryan didn't have to glance at his watch to know that the time was closing in on midnight.

Twelve midnight—that notorious hour when fairy tales came to an end and Cinderella went home for the night, leaving her prince standing alone in the dark.

Except Evangeline wasn't looking at him with goodbye in her eyes. When she turned her gaze on him beneath the golden glow of the Village lamplights, he saw an unmistakable hint of something else. A new beginning.

"Ryan." For the first time since she'd walked through the revolving door of the Bennington, she didn't utter his name as if it were a curse word. On the contrary, it sounded more like a plea.

Something stirred deep inside him. Remembrance.

She whispered his name again, just as she had the last time she'd led him up these stairs.

"Eve," he said before he could stop himself, cupping her face in his hands.

Conviction churned in his gut. He knew good and well it was time to turn around and walk away. He shouldn't be letting her lift her arms and drape them languidly around his neck. His hands shouldn't be dropping to her waist, settling on the graceful dip just above her womanly hips. And he sure as hell had no business growing hard.

But he was. He was as hard as granite, and he'd barely touched her.

Step away. Do it now, while you still can.

He'd have given all he had—his shares in the Bennington, his penthouse overlooking Central Park and all the other pointless material possessions he'd accumulated—just to have her again. To hear her whisper his name on a broken sigh as he drove himself inside her.

What *things* matter, anyway? He'd spent a lifetime trying to make something of himself, trying to prove that he was better than his absentee parents... more than just the sum of their parts. Where had it gotten him?

Alone, that's where.

But he didn't just want Evangeline's body. He wanted…

More.

He wanted things he hadn't let himself want in a very long time. Since before the whole fiasco with Natalie. Things he wasn't prepared to want again. As ugly as the end had been between them, there'd been a certain sense of poetic justice in their parting. Only a fool wouldn't have seen it. Ryan didn't deserve the things he'd once wanted so desperately. He wouldn't have known what to do with them even if he'd had them.

Thanks for that, Mom and Dad.

Evangeline shifted, her breasts brushing softly against his chest. She gazed up at him through the lush fringe of her lashes, and her lips parted ever so slightly.

Don't. Don't ask me.

His thoughts were screaming even as his erection swelled, his mind and body in a full-on war with one another. To his great shame, he wasn't sure which would emerge victorious.

Please don't.

Evangeline rose up on tiptoe and every muscle in his frame tensed as her mouth hovered irresistibly close to his ear.

"Kiss me," she murmured, her breath dancing softly against his jaw.

How could he refuse?

He wanted her. There was no denying it. She knew it as well as he did, or she never would have dared to ask him for a kiss.

She's going to hate you after tonight. Rightfully so.

Her eyes were already closed, as her face tipped upward toward his. Then her mouth was just a whisper away, ready...wanting...

All he had to do was lean in and touch his lips to hers. One taste and he'd be a goner. No turning back.

He slid one hand along her jaw, pausing to brush the pad of his thumb gently along the swell of her lower lip before taking her chin in his grasp so that when her eyes fluttered open she was looking directly at him.

She blinked. Impatience creased her brow.

"We can't," he said as evenly as he could manage. "Not now. Not yet."

She blinked again, confused for a moment, as if he'd spoken to her in a foreign language. The moment was so bittersweet that Ryan wanted to swallow his words. Take them back and crush his mouth to hers.

He could practically feel her lips, cold from the biting wind, taste the forbidden warmth of her tongue sliding against his.

But it was too late.

"Oh my God." She shook her head, incredulous. "*Oh my God.* We can't? After everything you said to me tonight?"

He held up his hands. "Eve, let me explain."

"Don't call me that," she spit. "Ever again."

He nodded. "I deserve that."

It stung, nonetheless.

"You deserve worse. You told me to ask you when I wanted you to kiss me, so I did. And then you *refuse*?" She shook her head, blinking furiously as her eyes grew shiny with unshed tears. "Is this just some kind of game to you?"

"It's not what you think," he said, reaching for her.

She stepped backward, out of his grasp. "Is this something you do with all your other women? Are you playing hard to get, playboy-style?"

Ryan paused, and his jaw clenched with enough force to grind coal into diamonds. "First of all, there are no other women."

She rolled her eyes.

He sighed, not bothering to remind her she shouldn't believe everything she read in the papers, as she'd so clearly already made up her mind about him.

He narrowed his gaze. "Second of all, I don't play games. I'm a grown man, unlike..." *Him*.

He couldn't bring himself to utter Jeremy's name.

She lifted a brow. "Don't tell me Manhattan's hottest bachelor is jealous."

"I'm most certainly not." He most certainly *was*. Far more than he wanted to admit, even to himself. *Damn it*. "You and I both know that if I kiss you right now, it won't end there. Are you ready for that, Evangeline?"

He stepped closer, backing her up against the brick wall of her building, and planted his hands on either side of her head, hemming her in.

She stared daggers at him but couldn't seem to form a response. How on earth this woman could believe she wasn't passionate was a mystery he couldn't begin to fathom. She swallowed, drawing his attention to her neck, where her pulse boomed with such force he could see it flutter in the hollow of her throat. An excited little butterfly.

Lust shot through him, hard and fast. He needed to leave before he did something they'd both regret. But first she needed to know why he was willingly walking away from something they both wanted.

Needed. Craved.

He fixed his gaze on hers, staring into her eyes with such intention that she had no choice but to listen. "The last time I took you to bed, you were there because another man told you some things that were not only cruel, but also flat-out wrong. Maybe that wasn't the only reason, but it was certainly one of them. And that was fine. *Then.* I'm not judging your decision process in the slightest. We hardly knew each other. We were strangers."

She crossed her arms, but her hot gaze never strayed from his.

He continued, "Now I know you, Evangeline. I know you, and I want you now more than ever before. Hear what I'm saying—I want you so much that the next time I make love to you, there will be no one else in your head. Or your heart."

He swallowed. His throat felt raw all of a sudden, his words like razors scraping away at his deepest regret.

Maybe his refusal to kiss her wasn't as much about Jeremy as it was to do with Natalie. Either way, he was doing the right thing. Neither of them had a place here.

"The next time I kiss you...the next time I take

you to bed…it will be about us. And only us. Just you and me." His voice cracked on his parting words. "That's a promise."

Chapter Eight

In a perfect world, Evangeline would have called in sick the next day in order to avoid having to face her bachelor boss.

But she didn't live in a perfect world. She lived in a crazy, mixed-up place where Jeremy had become a culinary superstar without even trying, where she'd resorted to sneaking her dogs out in the middle of the night to do their business and worst of all, where she'd humiliated herself by asking Ryan to kiss her, only to have him adamantly refuse.

No.

He'd said *no.*

She couldn't believe it. *He'd* been the one who'd planted the idea in her head in the first place. *He'd* been the one who'd held her hand in the restaurant and given her that stirring speech about how passionate she was. And then he'd turned her down flat.

It was mortifying. Worse than mortifying. She'd never been so embarrassed in her life. Not even when Jeremy had confessed his affair.

She wouldn't have admitted as much to anyone, of course, least of all Ryan Wilde. She'd known the man for less than two months. She absolutely shouldn't be more emotional about his dismissal than she was about a breakup with someone she'd dated for two years.

And yet, she was.

Because he'd been right. She hadn't wanted just a kiss. She'd wanted more. She'd wanted all of him. Again. And he'd been fully aware of her intentions. He'd stood there and looked her right in the eyes as she'd yearned for him, burning with desire while snow fell around them, dusting his hair in a fine veil of frosty white.

Then he'd turned her down.

He'd framed his refusal in a promise, but Evangeline knew a rejection when she heard one.

Now, in the cold light of day, she was almost grateful. Sleeping with him again would have been a massive mistake. Nothing was going to change the fact that he was her boss. He also moonlighted as an expert playboy, apparently. And he was so skilled at it that he managed to trick women into throwing themselves at him, Evangeline included.

God, it was nauseating. She felt a sudden stab of sympathy for the Ryan Wilde fan club that gathered in the hotel lobby every morning. Bile rose to the back of her throat as she rounded the corner near Grand Central Station and the Bennington came into view.

The irony of her predicament wasn't lost on her. She legitimately felt physically ill, but calling in sick wasn't an option. She wouldn't have Ryan thinking she couldn't handle seeing him again. She preferred him to stop thinking about her at all, actually.

And vice versa.

Note taken, self.

"Good afternoon, Miss Holly." The general manager greeted her from behind the reservation desk as she clicked across the expansive lobby in her highest stilettos.

Power shoes.

"Good afternoon, Elliot." Her stomach churned, but she ignored it and shot him her brightest smile.

I might have begged my boss to kiss me last night, but I'm a professional, darn it.

Elliot's gaze flitted toward the hallway beyond the elevator bank. "Mr. Wilde would like to see you in the conference room adjacent to his office."

Her smile froze into place. *I'll bet he would.*

She shook her head. "I can't. I have a meeting with a vendor in half an hour. Would you let him know, please?"

Elliot frowned. "I'm afraid he's rearranged his schedule and stayed late specifically to meet with you and the other Mr. Wilde."

"Oh." He was talking about Zander, not Ryan. She really wished one of them would change his last name so she would stop getting them mixed up. "I see. Of course I'll make myself available."

Her tummy gave another sickening flip. Zander

had rearranged his day in order to meet with her and Ryan the minute she walked in the door?

He knows.

Her humiliation was multiplied one hundred times over. Was she about to get grilled about her personal life? Was Zander going to make her explain the awkward events of the night before?

Was she about to be *fired*?

She couldn't lose this job. She had an elderly grandfather and two dogs depending on her.

Relax. You've done nothing wrong.

True, thanks to Ryan's sudden virtuous streak.

Still, her faith in her power shoes was beginning to waver. She swallowed and pressed a hand to her stomach as she neared the conference room.

"Hello, Evangeline. Come on in." Zander waved at the empty chair beside Ryan when she poked her head inside the door.

She'd have preferred to sit someplace else. *Any-place* else, actually. But at least she wouldn't have to look at him.

She lowered herself into the designated seat. Ryan's gaze swept over her, but she kept her attention fixed firmly forward.

Zander sat back in his chair, a little too relaxed for a CEO who was about to fire someone. "Well?" he prompted. "How was last night? Give me the debrief."

Evangeline released a breath she hadn't realized she'd been holding. This was a simple discussion about Mon Ami Jules, not a termination. She could do this. Easy-peasy.

Where shall I start? With the fact that the chef was

*my ex or the part where a tiny brush of Ryan's thumb
against the palm of my hand gave me goose bumps?*

"The wine was substandard," she said flatly.

"I disagree," Ryan countered with a lazy shrug.

Of course he did. Would it kill him to cooperate
with her on one tiny thing? Especially when that
thing was her area of expertise?

Zander frowned and consulted the stack of papers
spread across the table in front of him. "I've got a
copy of Carlo Bocci's review for the *Times*, and he
specifically mentions the excellence of the sommelier's recommendation."

He glanced at the printed page on top of the stack
again. "It was a Côtes du Rhône."

Evangeline asked him to name the vintage, and
he rattled off the information that matched the wine
the sommelier had poured for her and Ryan the night
before.

"Interesting." She pulled a face. "I wasn't particularly impressed with it."

Zander's attention shifted toward Ryan. "But you
liked it?"

"I did," he said slowly. "But I'm not the expert."

That's right. You're not.

But Carlo Bocci sort of was, and he disagreed
with her, too.

Evangeline's smile grew tight. She wished they'd
move on to a critique of the meal. But now that she
thought about it, she'd barely eaten anything. She
hadn't had much of an appetite lately.

"Do we have this wine in-house?" Zander asked.

Evangeline nodded. "Yes, we do. Would you like
me to pour a glass for you?"

Zander held up three fingers. "Pour one for each of us. I think a tasting is in order."

"Very well. I'll be right back."

It was a relief to escape the room for a few minutes, even though she was beginning to feel like her job was indeed on the line. Her taste was being questioned. That's what was happening, wasn't it?

Fine. She had the utmost confidence in her ability to evaluate wines. She'd grown up surrounded by grapevines. She knew wine like the back of her hand. More so than Carlo Bocci, probably.

She returned to the conference room holding a decanter, a trio of balloon-style wineglasses and a bottle of the red in question. Once she'd placed the items on the conference table, she gave Zander and Ryan a brief lesson on Côtes du Rhône varieties. If she was going to present a wine for tasting, she insisted on doing it right. Like a proper sommelier, because that's what she was.

For the time being, anyway.

"A good Côtes du Rhône will never upstage a meal, but was instead created to enhance it," she said. "It's a fruit-driven, quiet wine. Medium-bodied with an earthy flavor."

She uncorked the bottle, and to her great dismay, realized that her hands were shaking. She blamed Ryan. His unwavering stare as she spoke was beginning to unnerve her. She felt exposed...vulnerable, as if she were standing naked at the head of the table.

"Are you feeling okay, Evangeline?" Zander asked. "You look rather pale."

She glanced up from the bottle in her hands, her

rebellious gaze veering straight toward Ryan. His brow was creased in concern.

"I'm fine, thank you." *I'm blowing this.*

Her original plan had been to stick to her guns and convince them she was right. The wine was bad, plain and simple, even though she ordinarily enjoyed a nice glass of CDR. And the vineyard that had produced this vintage had a sterling reputation.

She realized now that she was going to have to switch gears. Bocci was a Michelin star reviewer. *The* reviewer who'd hopefully be dining at Bennington 8 sometime in the coming weeks. Arguing against his opinion would be pointless.

She was going to have to fake it. She'd sip the wine and pretend it was the best Côtes du Rhône she'd ever tasted. It was her only option.

Easier said than done.

When she poured the wine into the decanter so it could breathe, she was hit with an aroma so strong that it nearly knocked her over. Fermented grapes, black plum, candied berries—she could smell it all. And everything seemed...*off.* The fruity notes were so pungent they almost smelled rotten. When she swallowed, she tasted vinegar at the back of her throat.

She covered her mouth with her free hand in an effort to stop herself from gagging. Something was wrong. Very, very wrong. Côtes du Rhône shouldn't have such a strong bouquet, even if it had somehow gone bad. It wasn't a heavy wine. Many experts called it cabernet light.

There was nothing light about the overwhelming smell of alcohol burning Evangeline's nostrils. She forced herself to breathe only through her mouth as she swirled the wine in the decanter so it could properly aerate.

"Evangeline." The silence in the conference room was broken by Ryan aggressively clearing his throat. "Can I see you in private for a moment?"

Seriously?

She stared at him and shook her head as subtly as she could manage.

No. Absolutely not.

Zander glanced back and forth between them. "What is it, Ryan?"

Ryan's gaze remained steadfastly fixed on Evangeline's face when he answered. "It's personal."

She was going to kill him. She was going to strangle him with his fancy Hermès tie right then and there.

"I'm sorry, Zander. I have no idea what he's talking about." A hysterical laugh bubbled up her throat. *Get it together.* She addressed Ryan without bothering to look at him. "I'm sure whatever you need to discuss with me can wait until after the tasting."

"It can't," he countered.

She pretended not to hear him as she poured three glasses, sliding two of them across the table toward the men.

Zander kept glancing around, appeared thoroughly confused, albeit handsomely so. The Wilde family had clearly lucked out in the genetic lottery.

"Evangeline," Ryan said tersely.

"Ryan." She pasted a smile on her face and fixed her gaze with his. *Would you kindly shut up?*

Zander held up his glass. "Cheers?" It sounded more like a question than a proper toast.

Evangeline reached for her drink, more than ready to get the tasting over with. She had no intention of speaking to Ryan one-on-one afterward. If he thought she was going to discuss anything remotely personal with him at work, he'd lost his arrogant mind.

She didn't *ever* want to speak to him alone again, and definitely wouldn't be asking him to kiss her again. No. Way. She just wanted to forget last night ever happened.

A glass of wine suddenly seemed like an excellent idea, even though the smell made her stomach turn. But just as her fingertips were about to make contact with the crystal stem of her wineglass, Ryan reached for it, too. It almost seemed as if he did it on purpose, she thought.

Red wine splashed all over her, from the cowl-necked top of her white angora sweater to the tips of her suddenly drenched power stilettos. As she stood there with Côtes du Rhône dripping from her hair, a wave of nausea hit her hard and fast, and she no longer cared whether or not the spill had been intentional. She needed to get to a bathroom.

Immediately.

She'd worry about pummeling Ryan Wilde later.

Well, that didn't turn out quite like I planned.

Ryan closed his eyes. Took a deep breath. When he opened them, red wine was dripping from the conference table onto the plush dove-gray carpet.

Zander was looking at him as if he'd just sprouted another head.

Evangeline was nowhere to be seen.

"Sorry," he said. "We reached for the same glass and…"

He didn't bother finishing. There was no way Zander would buy such a flimsy explanation. Not when every visible surface was drenched in Côtes du Rhône.

He'd panicked. He'd never intended to make such a mess. *Obviously*. He'd just wanted to stop Evangeline from taking a sip.

Mission accomplished, idiot.

"I should go check on Miss Holly." He turned and headed for the door.

He couldn't get into a discussion with Zander about this disaster. Not now. He could barely think straight, let alone come up with a reasonable excuse for his behavior.

He'd explain everything eventually. If what he suspected was true, he wouldn't have a choice.

"Send for housekeeping while you're at it, would you?" Zander said calmly.

Too calmly.

"Will do." Ryan strode out of the room.

He flagged down the closest hotel employee and requested help in the conference room, then headed for the nearby ladies' room. He didn't linger. Didn't think twice about what to do next. He ignored the feminine stick figure sign and pushed his way inside.

By some miracle, the restroom was empty, save for one stall with its door closed. He settled against the marble counter, crossed his arms and waited.

Sure enough, Evangeline emerged seconds later, looking as white as a sheet. Ryan's heart gave an undeniable tug. She was like a very lovely ghost of her very lovely self. Pale, fragile, delicate. All words he normally wouldn't associate with Evangeline.

Then she caught sight of him and managed to muster enough strength to narrow her eyes in fury.

"Get out," she croaked.

He shook his head. "We need to talk. Now."

"Do you have any idea how crazy you're behaving? You just tossed a glass of wine at me, and now you've ambushed me in the women's restroom." She waved her arms around the restroom's serene interior. "Is it even legal for you to be here?"

He didn't know. Nor did he care.

"I'm sorry about your clothes. I'll replace them with whatever you'd like. Take my Bloomingdale's card." He started to reach for the inside pocket of his suit jacket, then stopped.

What was he doing? He'd barged in here because he had something to say. Something important. Something that would change her life in a profound way. His, too, possibly.

If what he suspected was true.

How could this be happening again?

Sitting beside Zander while Evangeline poured the wine, struggling not to gag, Ryan had a deep sense of déjà vu. He was being revisited by his deepest desire and his worst nightmare, all rolled into one. Of course he'd panicked. It was a wonder he'd managed to hold on to anything remotely resembling sanity.

"Save it. I don't want your money. I just want you to let me do my job." Evangeline lifted her chin in defiance, but there was a telltale wobble in her bottom lip that told him that wasn't *all* she wanted. Like him, she wanted more. But for some reason, she couldn't bring herself to admit it.

The urge to close the distance between them and take her in his arms was overwhelming.

He didn't dare.

The door to the restroom flew open, and a woman holding a little girl by the hand stepped inside.

The young girl's eyes went as big as saucers. "Mommy, why is there a man in here?"

Ryan's throat clogged. *Mommy.*

He sighed mightily and tried his best not to look like a weirdo who cornered women in restrooms on a regular basis. "I'm sorry. Could you give us a minute? Please?"

After casting a questioning glance toward Evangeline, the girl's mother seemed satisfied nothing untoward was going on. She nodded. "Fine. One minute. But we'll be right outside."

"Thank you." He scrubbed a hand over his face. Super. Now he was being timed.

Once they were alone again, Evangeline strode to the sink, wet a paper towel and pressed it to her forehead. She closed her eyes and her voice dropped to a raw whisper. "I might need to go home for a while. I think I'm coming down with something."

Ryan watched as she tossed the paper towel in the trash and stared at her reflection in the mirror.

She wrapped her arms around herself, like she was trying as hard as she could to hold herself together. Her gaze dropped lower, and Ryan's heart lodged firmly in his throat as her hand slid to her stomach.

Surely she knew.

He couldn't be the only one. All the signs were there—the nausea, the fatigue. Hadn't he seen her nodding off in the wine cooler a few days ago?

But the clincher was her sudden aversion to alcohol. No one loved wine more than Evangeline. Ryan had never met anyone so knowledgeable or passionate about the stuff.

And yet she'd turned her nose up at every glass she'd come across in the past week. Somewhere on his desk he had a copy of an irate email from a vendor who'd written to him to complain that Evangeline had refused delivery on a case of Bordeaux shipped all the way from France because the wine had allegedly turned sour. It was a wonder he hadn't figured out what was going on days ago.

He hadn't suspected a thing until moments ago in the conference room when she'd opened the bottle of red and looked as though she might faint. The truth had hit him like a ton of bricks, and now it was so obvious that he couldn't believe he hadn't seen it sooner.

On some level, she had to know, too.

All that was left was for one of them to say it.

He took a deep breath and met her gaze in the mirror. "Evangeline, you're not sick. You're pregnant."

Chapter Nine

Pregnant.

Pregnant!

How could she have let this happen?

It was official. She was an abysmal failure at one-night stands. She would never, ever have one again. One little slip, and now her entire life had changed.

"No." She shook her head. "I can't be."

She'd missed her period last month, but not entirely. There'd been some spotting and even a little bit of cramping. Granted, she'd been tired a lot. And there'd been that strange night at wine group the other day when she hadn't been able to identify a single vintage. She hadn't had much of a taste for wine at all lately.

"Eve." Ryan's tone had suddenly gone so quiet, so serious, that she couldn't bring herself to chastise him again for calling her by the name she now associated with her adventurous, sexy alter ego...that passionate fool.

He was right, wasn't he? He hadn't needed to say it. The truth had slammed right into her right around the time she'd fallen to her knees in front of the toilet bowl—she was pregnant. She just hadn't wanted to believe it.

She had all the early symptoms. Every single one of them.

"It's going to be okay." Ryan's mouth curved into a tiny smile. "I promise."

He was *smiling*? At a time like this?

She tore her gaze from the mirror and turned to face him. Her knees wobbled, and she had to grip the counter behind her to steady herself, but something about the subtle lift of his lips took the edge off her panic.

Until some semblance of clarity descended on her and she fully grasped what his smile meant—the baby growing inside her wasn't just hers. It was his. She was pregnant with Ryan Wilde's child.

She shook her head. Hard. "We don't even know if it's true. It could be the flu. I need to see a doctor."

Maybe multiple doctors. A whole team of medical professionals. She needed to be sure before she could begin to wrap her head around this.

A baby.

Ryan's baby.

There was no doubt in her mind. She'd never been as amorous with Jeremy as she'd been that night with Ryan. She couldn't even remember the last time she and Jeremy had slept together, which should probably have been a warning sign that the relationship wasn't all she'd believed it to be.

Now here she was, possibly pregnant by a man with whom she had no relationship whatsoever.

She studied him, marveling at his composure. How was he so calm? Aside from drenching her in Côtes du Rhône, he seemed completely unruffled.

The wine.

She let her gaze travel to his hands, his fingertips, and she stared, remembering the way he knocked the glass out of her grasp...the unmistakable intention in his eyes. He'd deliberately stopped her from drinking because he'd suspected she was pregnant and he'd been worried about the baby.

It was sweet, in a controlling, maniacal sort of way. But it still didn't mean she was actually pregnant, and it definitely didn't mean she was chomping at the bit to start a family with him. Or anyone.

"I doubt it's the flu," he said evenly. "But seeing a doctor is a good idea. I'll ring the driver."

He gathered his cell phone from his pocket, but before he could dial, Evangeline grabbed his wrist. "Wait a minute. How are you so intimately acquainted with early-pregnancy symptoms?"

His expression went blank. Guarded.

Oh God.

"I see." She swallowed, and a fresh wave of nausea rolled over her. "You've been through this before."

Of course he had. How naive could she be? The man had a literal harem. There were probably tiny Ryan Wildes running around all over Manhattan.

She released her hold on his wrist and brushed a tear from the corner of her eye. She hadn't even realized she'd started to cry. And when had her hands begun to tremble so violently? Her body felt as though it was crumpling in on itself.

"Have I been through this before? Yes and no," he said after a long pause.

What did that even mean?

The bathroom door swung open again, revealing the young mother who'd tried to enter moments ago. She narrowed her gaze at Ryan and planted her free hand on her hip. Her tiny daughter maintained a firm grip on the other one. "It's been *three* minutes. Time's up. We're coming in."

Ryan held up his hands in a gesture of surrender. "My apologies. Do come in."

They had a brief conversation, wherein Ryan asked if she was a guest at the hotel and promised to have an extensive selection of complimentary desserts sent up to their room in return for her patience. Everything on the menu, from the Italian cream cake to the triple banana split. The little girl's eyes lit up, and her mother exchanged a few more words with Ryan.

Evangeline couldn't keep up with what was being said. All her attention was focused on the toddler— the bright red bow in her hair, her patent leather Mary Janes, the lace trim on her ankle socks. But above all else, Evangeline couldn't stop marveling at the way she never let go of her mother's hand.

She inhaled a shuddering breath. Fate had made some kind of terrible mistake. Evangeline didn't know the first thing about being a mother. The very word was almost foreign to her.

"Let's go." Ryan wrapped his hand around her waist

and ushered her out the door, toward the Bennington lobby.

She wanted to tell him not to touch her. Pregnancy aside, she still wasn't over the humiliating events of the night before. Plus they were at work. Zander was probably back in the conference room, mopping up wine and getting termination papers in order for both of them. The usual crowd of blushing bachelorettes was gathered beneath the massive gold clock that hung above the sitting area's sumptuous velvet sofas, beaming at Ryan as they walked past.

But Evangeline didn't protest. It had been a long time since she'd had anyone to lean on. A very long, very lonely time. And even though she knew she shouldn't—even though she was painfully aware that they weren't a real couple and never would be—she rested her head against his broad shoulder and let him bear the weight of her burdened heart.

Just this once.

Ryan had Tony take them to the closest urgent care center. A hospital seemed like overkill, but the likelihood of getting an appointment with a regular doctor in Manhattan on the spur of the moment was dubious at best. Evangeline sat beside him, growing paler by the minute as she stared out the limousine's window.

A baby.

Ryan's chest seized. He took a deep inhale, but the limo felt short on air all of a sudden.

Could he do this again? Could he hold Evangeline's hand through nine months of doctor's appointments, attend birthing classes and cater to her nutty pregnancy cravings?

Could he open his home and his heart to an infant? *This won't be like last time. It can't.*

He couldn't possibly be that unlucky twice in a lifetime. Then again, his present circumstances didn't have anything to do with luck. He'd chosen Evangeline that night. He'd known next to nothing about her, but he'd broken every rule he'd lived by since the Natalie fiasco and taken her to bed. He wasn't altogether certain he'd used a condom either. That was a definite first.

A shrink would probably tell him he'd chosen these circumstances, that a part of him still longed for the family he never had as a boy. A real family, a mom and dad instead of an aunt and uncle who'd been kind enough to take him in when he'd had no-where else to go. Hell, Zander would probably say the same thing.

He'd be wrong.

Ryan knew better than to reach for things he'd never had. He'd wanted Evangeline. He still did, now more than ever. But wanting her…needing her… wasn't the same as believing they could have for-ever. He'd accepted his fate. Having a family, a life, ripped out from under you not once, but twice, did that to a person.

The car slowed to a stop in front of a small build-ing just off Madison with a red cross in the window and a sign indicating no appointment necessary.

Tony met Ryan's gaze in the rearview mirror. "Shall I wait here, sir?"

Evangeline grasped the door handle closest to her, ready to bolt. "That's not necessary. I can take it from here."

"No," Ryan countered. Over his dead body. "I'll accompany Miss Holly, Tony. Stand by and I'll give you a call when we're finished."

"Yes, sir."

Evangeline sighed, but didn't put up more of a fight. Ryan suspected she was probably too preoccupied to argue, and for that he was grateful.

Once inside, Evangeline explained to the receptionist that she needed a pregnancy test. A *blood* test, she specified. The most reliable one available. The woman on the other side of the frosted glass partition nodded and handed her a clipboard full of forms, which Evangeline completed at warp speed despite her trembling hands.

A nurse in scrubs called her back almost immediately. At the sound of Evangeline's name, Ryan stood.

Evangeline squeezed his hand, but at the same time said, "No. Please. I'd like to do this on my own."

Then she was gone.

The door clicked closed behind her, and he found himself alone in the sterile waiting room, shut out and enveloped in antiseptic odors and the monotonous, even beeps of medical equipment. Sights, sounds and smells that were all too familiar.

He'd been in a waiting room eerily similar to this one when he'd learned the truth. When the grand charade had fallen apart. Natalie had given birth just five hours previously, and at first, everything seemed fine. Not just fine—wonderful. Better than Ryan ever imagined.

He and Natalie had only been seeing each other for four months when she'd told him she was expecting. To say it had been a shock would be a massive understatement. He'd been so careful. But there wasn't a birth control method on earth that was one hundred percent effective, and even though it would have been a stretch to say he and Natalie were in love, they were going to be parents. Together.

Letting her raise the baby alone was never an option. Ryan couldn't fathom the thought of not being a part of his child's day-to-day life. He moved in with Natalie right away, and he was there for every moment of the pregnancy—every bout of morning sickness, every sonogram.

Then came the contractions. The birth. And Ryan was there for that, too, squeezing Natalie's hand and urging her to push. The moment the baby boy's cries pierced the air, something had come loose inside Ryan—some part of him that had been bound up tight, cutting off his oxygen since the day his parents had abandoned him and left him to fend for himself at six years of age.

He could breathe again, and the future seemed so blindingly bright. A shimmering, soulful place where he had someone to call his own. He remembered with absolute clarity sitting in that hospital lounge—the one that so resembled the polished, sanitary space where he sat now—with his head in his hands, overcome with relief. As soon as he'd seen that baby, heard his plaintive cries, Ryan had loved that child. The doubts he'd had all along about Natalie didn't seem to matter anymore. They could raise the baby together. They could be a family, and love would come. Eventually.

Then came the hand, heavy on his shoulder, and the look of alarm on the doctor's face—the same doctor who'd just smiled at Ryan in the delivery room minutes before. *It's a boy.*

Ryan had known right away that something had gone terribly wrong. There was no misinterpreting that expression. He tried to ask for specifics, but the words stuck in his throat.

"The baby is in distress," the doctor bluntly stated.

After Ryan had stepped out of the room to call Zander and the rest of the Wildes, the baby had started bleeding internally. They'd stopped the hemorrhage right away but as a result he'd become severely anemic.

"Is there anything I can do?" Ryan had asked once he'd regained the ability to form words. "Donate blood, maybe?"

"That would be a huge help. In cases of neonatal transfusions, we try to use direct donations from family members as much as we can."

So Ryan had gone straight to the hospital's blood lab, and that's where he learned that Natalie's baby—the tiny little boy he'd fallen in love with on sight, the family he'd never had—wasn't his, after all.

His blood wasn't a match. Both Natalie and her son had O negative blood type, and Ryan's blood was AB positive. It was medically impossible for him to be the father.

Natalie had known the truth all along. Once the baby was out of the woods and she was presented with the irrefutable evidence, she'd confessed.

She never apologized, never shed a tear. "I wanted you to be the father. Shouldn't that count for something?"

With those words, the best day of Ryan's life had become the worst.

The crazy thing was, he might have still stuck around. He'd anticipated the birth of that baby for months. But Natalie didn't wait for him to decide. When he showed up at the hospital the following morning to talk things out with her, she'd packed up her son and gone.

"Can I get you anything, sir?"

Ryan looked up. The nurse who'd just escorted Evangeline to the back of the urgent care clinic stood a few feet away with a bottle of water in one hand and a steaming disposable cup in the other.

"You looked so worried, I thought you could use a distraction." She held both offerings toward him.

"Thank you." He chose the coffee. It was terrible, but he was grateful nonetheless.

"You're welcome. And don't worry. Your wife will be out in just a few minutes." She padded away, her white sneakers squishing softly on the polished tile floor.

Your wife.

The words echoed in Ryan's consciousness. He waited for the inevitable tightness in his chest that usually came when someone mentioned his name in the same breath as marriage. It happened on a surprisingly frequent basis, most notably on the pages of Vows, the *New York Times*' wedding section.

He usually laughed it off. Made a joke out of it, which was undoubtedly why Zander thought hanging the Hottest Bachelor magazine cover in his office was hilarious.

But he didn't feel much like laughing now. Nor

did his chest feel like it was being squeezed in a vise. For reasons he didn't want to examine too closely, he felt fine. Happy, almost.

Which defied all logic.

He was losing it, he thought bitterly as he sipped his coffee. Evangeline emerged moments later, just as he choked down the dregs. Their gazes locked, and he stood.

"You were right." She took a deep breath, and then her hand slid to her stomach and settled there in a protective gesture that rendered her following words unnecessary. "The test was positive. I'm pregnant."

Chapter Ten

She was going to have to quit her job.

Obviously.

It wasn't as if she could be an effective sommelier if she couldn't even drink wine. Although she knew her pregnancy wouldn't last forever. And she could always use a tasting spit cup. Sommeliers did it all the time, but something told her Zander Wilde would be less than thrilled to know his wine director was expelling every sip she took into an empty glass. Even if the empty glass was Baccarat cut crystal, which was what sat on every table at Bennington 8.

Besides, at the moment Evangeline couldn't tolerate even the smallest whiff of alcohol, much less the taste of it. So, the morning after the surreal visit to the urgent care clinic, she typed her letter of resignation and then strode into the Bennington with it tucked neatly into her handbag.

She glanced at the sitting area where Ryan's fan club usually assembled, but for once it was unoccupied. The little zing of relief that fluttered through her told her the resignation letter in her bag had less to do with her ability to do her job and everything to do with the father of her baby.

She couldn't work with Ryan day in and day out while his unborn child grew inside her. She just couldn't. It was hardly professional, but more than that, it was just plain dangerous.

She'd practically thrown herself at him before she knew she was pregnant. How was she supposed to maintain her distance from him now? When he'd turned her down before, she'd been embarrassed. But there was more at stake now than her pride. So much more. Now she had everything to lose.

A future.

A family.

Her heart.

The ride home from the urgent care clinic had been excruciating. No one had said a word, which Evangeline took to understand that Ryan wouldn't argue when she handed him the letter and told him she thought they should go their separate ways. He'd probably be relieved.

Neither of them had planned this pregnancy. Neither of them wanted it. Except now that it was happening, Evangeline *did* want it. She wanted the baby—her baby, *Ryan's* baby—very much. More than she'd wanted anything in as long as she could remember.

She didn't know a thing about being a mother. Her own mom hadn't exactly been a stellar example. But if her own childhood had taught her anything, it was that her baby came first. From here on out, all of her focus had to be on her pregnancy. Potentially getting her heart crushed by the bachelor of the year didn't belong anywhere in the equation.

She took a deep breath as she rounded the corner and walked the remaining steps toward Ryan's office. She hadn't set foot inside the luxe space since her first day of work when she'd vowed to keep everything between them strictly business.

Epic fail.

"Ryan, I…" Her voice faltered when she stepped inside, looked around and found the office empty.

Great. He wasn't there. It had taken her an entire day's worth of pep talks to bring herself to face the playboy father of her baby, to say the things she needed to say, and he wasn't even there.

Maybe it was for the best. Maybe fate had finally cut her a break. She wasn't sure if she could go through with it if she had to look him in the eye while she pretended she wanted to have the baby all on her own.

She didn't.

But she also didn't want to end up like her father had after her mother left.

Losing her had broken him. Evangeline didn't want to be broken like that. She'd spent her entire adult life protecting herself from that kind of pain. It was why she'd stayed with Jeremy as long as she had, even though deep down she'd always known she deserved something different. Something better. Something real.

It was also why she'd been in such a hurry to kick

Ryan out of her apartment when she'd woken up with his cuff links on her nightstand and her head on his chest. She couldn't be broken by the loss of something she'd never really had.

The letter inside her bag seemed like a terrible, living, breathing thing. Evangeline was eager to be rid of it, before she changed her mind. She reached for the crisp white envelope, crossed the spacious office and placed it on Ryan's chair. Right where he couldn't miss it.

She paused for a beat, and Ryan's words from the night outside her apartment danced in her mind, like a magical, mystical snowfall.

I want you so much that the next time I make love to you, there will be no one else in your head. Or your heart.

Just you and me.

But it would never be just the two of them. There were three of them now. Everything had changed.

I can't do this.

She couldn't walk away with her typed resignation letter as her only goodbye. That would make her no better than her mother.

She turned back for the envelope, but a voice stopped her in her tracks.

A woman's voice, calling out, "Knock knock!"

The singsong quality of the greeting turned Evangeline's stomach. This was obviously someone who was close enough to Ryan to feel comfortable strolling into his office in the middle of the day. And to top it off, she was beautiful—willowy thin and graceful, with a neck like a swan and masses of thick dark hair piled on her head in the kind of casually elegant updo that Evangeline had never managed to master.

"Oh, sorry." The woman glanced around the office, registering the absence of its occupant. "Ryan's not in?"

So this stunning person and Ryan were on a first-name basis. Evangeline wasn't the least bit surprised.

"No, he's not." A lump lodged in her throat. She couldn't have felt more like a third wheel if she'd plopped right down in the lobby with all the other members of the Ryan Wilde fan club.

"Can I give him a message for you?" She hated the way her voice wavered, betraying her emotion. Resigning was the right thing to do. She couldn't stay here and linger on the fringe like an extra on an episode of *The Bachelor*.

"Oh my God. You think I'm one of them, don't you?" The balletic stranger laughed. "You think I'm one of Ryan's women."

Evangeline felt sick. *Ryan's women.* "You're not?"

"No." She rolled her eyes. "God, no. Those women are delusional. Although you have to admire their persistence. And their optimism. As far as I know, Ryan hasn't even gone out on a date in close to a year."

Wait…*what*?

"But he's New York's hottest bachelor." Evangeline's face went hot. "At least that's what the magazine cover says."

She gestured toward the framed issue of *Gotham* hanging above his desk, but it wasn't there anymore. The wall was bare.

The dancer followed her gaze. "He took it down a

while ago. My husband gave it to him as a joke, but Ryan never found it quite as amusing as Zander did. Men, am I right?" She rolled her eyes.

The pieces were falling into place. Evangeline remembered hearing something about Zander's wife being a ballet teacher. "You're Allegra?"

She nodded and extended a lithe arm. "Allegra Wilde."

Evangeline shook her hand. "Nice to meet you. I'm Evangeline."

Allegra smiled. "Ah, so you're the wine director I've heard so much about."

She nodded. She was still the hotel wine director... for now, at least. "I'm not sure where Ryan is at the moment. I need to speak to him myself, actually."

Allegra's gaze ventured over her shoulder and landed on the envelope in Ryan's chair. "I stopped by to have lunch with Zander. I thought I'd poke my head in to tell Ryan hello and see if he's coming to Sunday dinner this weekend. It was nice to see him last week. He's kept to himself for way too long. Such a hermit."

Hermit? Was she serious?

Evangeline probably shouldn't be having this conversation. Scratch that—she definitely shouldn't. It felt like prying. And the fact that she was seriously tempted to interrogate one of Ryan's family members to get more information on his supposedly notorious love life was pathetic.

"That whole bachelor business is just something a reporter for the Vows column at the *Times* made up because she was looking for another big story after the Bennington Curse was proven to be bogus." Allegra's voice softened, and something in her gaze made Evangeline's heart skip a beat. "Ryan Wilde is no playboy. You know that, don't you?"

The Bennington Curse. It had been all over the internet a few months ago. Evangeline wasn't sure about the specifics, other than it had something to do with runaway brides. It had always sounded more like a Julia Roberts romcom than real life.

The story about Ryan, however, she'd bought. Hook, line and sinker.

It was just so believable. He was handsome, charming and kind. Beyond swoon worthy. Weeks after they'd met, he still remembered which eye Olive could see out of. He'd gone out of his way to make her feel special at Mon Ami Jules. If he hadn't been there, she never would have made it through the first course. And he'd been so desperate to stop her from drinking the Côtes du Rhone in the conference room—desperate to protect her baby. Their baby.

Even his hands were nice. Strong. Manly...as if they'd be perfectly capable of assembling complicated furniture. A crib, perhaps.

Who wouldn't want to marry him?

She swallowed around the lump that was rapidly forming in her throat.

No.

No, no, no.

She would *not* start thinking she had actual feelings for him. Because she didn't. She *couldn't*.

"Why are you telling me this?" she asked Allegra in a near whisper.

Allegra smiled. "Because it's the truth. And because it seems like something you needed to hear."

Allegra's attention flitted to the envelope again and then back to Evangeline. She looked her right in the eye for a long, silent moment—a moment in which Evangeline's heart fluttered wildly in her chest.

Then before Allegra turned to go, her gaze drifted lower...to Evangeline's hand resting lightly, unconsciously, on her stomach, where Ryan's child grew inside her.

Ryan returned to his office after his monthly accounting meeting to find Evangeline standing beside his desk. Her arms were crossed, and she had the same determined expression that she'd worn the last time she'd sashayed into his inner sanctum.

Back then, she'd come to tell him she wanted to keep things between them purely professional. Back then, she'd also been pregnant. They'd just been oblivious to that significant detail.

"Evangeline." A trickle of worry snaked its way down his spine. He knew that look. "To what do I owe the pleasure?"

He sat down on the corner of his desk and did his best to ignore the clench in his gut that told him she'd come to deliver another unpleasant ultimatum.

She'd been alarmingly quiet on the way home from the clinic the night before. Shell-shocked. He'd thought it best to give her some space—time to absorb the fact that she was going to be a mother. Of course they needed to talk about how they were going to proceed, but he hadn't wanted to push. After all, they had nearly nine months to figure things out.

Looking at her now, he realized his silence had been a mistake. A big one.

"Why didn't you tell me?" She looked him up and down, her gaze lingering briefly on his hands. Then she lifted her glittering eyes to his.

She was breathtaking, even in her anger. So beautiful that it took him a moment to respond.

"You're going to have to give me a hint here, love." Her cheeks flared deliciously pink at the endearment. "What didn't I tell you?"

She took a step closer to him, so close that he could feel the heat of her indignation...of the passion that she still didn't quite believe she possessed. A wave of desire crashed over Ryan. If he hadn't already been seated, he might have fallen to his knees.

"All this time you let me think you were some kind of womanizer. A swinging bachelor." She swallowed, drawing his attention to her slender neck, where her pulse boomed furiously at the base of her throat. "And you're not."

Swinging bachelor?

Other than Hugh Hefner, had anyone ever used that term nonironically? What kind of cad had she thought he was, exactly?

"You're upset," he said evenly.

"Of course I'm upset," she spit.

"Because I'm a decent guy." Ryan lifted a brow.

She was so adorably furious, full of fire and light, and she wasn't making a lick of sense. But it was killing him not to touch her, to take her in his arms and kiss the righteous smirk right off her face.

"Precisely. Yes." She blinked, then frowned and

shook her head. "I mean, no. Not because you're decent, exactly. It's just…"

It's just that she was pregnant. They were having a baby together, and her reaction to the news had progressed from shock to panic.

She's scared.

She's scared out of her mind, and she's pushing you away.

He swallowed, suddenly far more troubled than amused.

Don't let her.

He stood, closed the distance between them and took her face in his hands. She glanced over his shoulder, toward the opened office door. Anyone in the building could have walked in on them right then, but Ryan couldn't have cared less. Their days of hiding were numbered. The truth was bound to come out eventually.

Not that he had a full grasp himself on what exactly was happening between them. What *was* the truth? They were going to be parents, but was that the extent of it?

Not if he could help it.

"What is it that you're trying to tell me? Talk to me, Evangeline," he said.

She looked at him for a long, loaded moment, as if he were some kind of complicated puzzle she was trying to understand. Then her voice dropped to a fragile whisper. So fragile that something broke inside Ryan when she finally spoke. "I hardly know a thing about you, and I'm having your baby."

His baby…

His.

Warmth radiated through Ryan's body, starting at the center and spreading outward to the tips of his fingers and toes. *Mine*.

He let his forehead fall against Evangeline's and ran his thumb in gentle, soothing circles over her cheek. He could have stayed that way all day, breathing her in. The mother of his child. "That's easily fixable, Eve. If there's something you want to know, just ask me. I'm right here."

Her eyes went wide. Glowing. "I can ask you anything. Really?"

"Really." He pulled back and waited, wondering just how deep she wanted to go.

Evangeline bit her lip as her gaze flitted to the wall above his desk. "When did you take the *Gotham* cover down?"

"On your first day of work, right after you came in here reading me the riot act."

She bit her lip. "Why?"

"Because I could tell it upset you, and because I always despised it myself."

The corner of her mouth tipped into a quiet grin.

"At last, a smile. Right answer?" He raised a brow.

She nodded. "Right answer."

"What else? I know there are more questions swirling in that gorgeous head of yours." He reached to tuck a stray curl behind her ear, enjoying the new-found intimacy between them, hoping it would last.

She took a deep breath. "Yesterday on the way to the clinic, when I asked if you'd been through this before, you gave a cryptic answer—yes and no. What did that mean?"

Ryan grew still.

He never discussed Natalie and her baby. With anyone. The Wildes knew what had happened of course, but Ryan resisted Emily's many efforts to get him to "talk it out." He wanted to forget. He didn't want to talk about it, hence his prolonged absence from Sunday dinner.

But Evangeline needed to know, before she jumped to more conclusions.

"Last year, a woman I was seeing became pregnant. She told me the child was mine, but on the day the baby was born, I found out she'd lied. I wasn't the father. We parted ways afterward." He tried to keep his gaze locked with hers, but in the end he couldn't. He didn't need to look her in the eye to know what he'd see there—pity. And he didn't want pity from Evangeline.

He wanted more.

Her breath hitched audibly in her throat, and then her hands reached for his. "Oh my God, Ryan. That's terrible."

"It's in the past." He looked up, and to his infinite surprise and relief, there wasn't a trace of pity in her expression. Only a promise.

She took his hands and placed them low on her stomach where their unborn child was growing inside her, its heart beating beneath his fingertips. "This baby is yours, Ryan. I want you to know that, without a doubt."

He was holding life in his hands—a life they'd

made together. It may have been unintentional, but it was no mistake. It was fate. Destiny. And he couldn't shake the feeling that it was another chance, somehow. For both of them.

If only they could find their way back to each other again. "I know. I trust you."

He did.

Maybe that made him a fool. He preferred to think it made him an optimist, but he believed her. There wasn't a chance that the baby was Jeremy's. If it were, she wouldn't be here, desperately trying to know him better. She wouldn't have reached for his hand and gripped it like a lifeline during the strange, silent ride back to her apartment last night.

She wouldn't be looking at him right now with that wild combination of terror and desire in her eyes.

The yearning between them was palpable. He could feel it in the way she shivered beneath his touch as his hands moved from her tummy to her hips. Pulling her closer...and closer still...until she was nestled neatly between his thighs. Her fingertips brushed against his leg, and that's all it took. He went hard in an instant. He wanted their baby, but he also wanted *her*. He'd wanted her for weeks. No amount of doors slammed in his face could change that.

Kiss me.

The words floated between them, as tender and lovely as snow caressing the treetops in Central Park.

"Eve," he said, clutching the fabric of her pencil skirt in his grip. Desperate. Devoted. "Is there something else you'd like to ask me?"

He'd promised his lips wouldn't touch hers until

she asked for it, and he was keeping his word. The pregnancy didn't change the fact that he wanted her to be ready. He wanted her to want him as badly as he wanted her. He wanted her to be *his*.

"Ryan." Her gaze dropped to his mouth, and his erection swelled.

He took a deep breath and forced himself to focus. To wait for her to ask. Then, in an effort to stop himself from crushing his mouth to hers prematurely, his gaze strayed over her shoulder.

That's when he finally saw it—a plain white envelope sitting in his chair.

His name had been printed on the front of it in feminine hand. Not just his first name, but his surname as well—Ryan Wilde—as if it had been left there by a stranger.

But it hadn't. He knew exactly where it had come from, and he was fairly sure he knew what was inside.

His hands stilled on her hips just as her lips parted, poised to say the words he'd been waiting for.

"Evangeline." His voice was hushed and flat, yet it sliced through the office like a knife. "What is that?"

She froze for a moment, her brow crumpling in confusion…and just a little bit of hurt.

Despite the spike of irritation that had hit him hard in the chest when he spotted the envelope, he registered the distress in her gaze. And a very real part of him hated himself for putting it there.

But the other part of him—the tender part, the damaged part, the part that needed to know she was *all in* before they went down this road again—was livid.

Her head spun slowly around, following his gaze. A second passed, maybe two. But they were among the longest seconds of Ryan's life. When she faced him again, the desire in her eyes had melted into something else. Regret, laced with a hint of fear.

"Tell me you didn't come in here while I was out and leave a resignation letter on my chair," Ryan said through gritted teeth.

"I didn't." Evangeline shook her head. "Well, I did. But it wasn't like that. I…"

Ryan knew he should give her a chance to explain. He knew she was scared. But damn it, so was he. Couldn't she see that? From the moment he'd woken up in her bed, she'd been pulling away from him, and she was still doing it. Only now, things were different. Now if she fled, she'd be taking their baby with her.

"Do you have any idea how finding a letter like that would have felt?" he said.

She shook her head. "But I wasn't going to leave it there. That's why I stayed. I…"

"Excuse me," someone said from the direction of the office door. It was followed by a pointed clearing of a throat.

Evangeline, still standing between Ryan's legs, flew backward, as far away as she could get.

"I apologize for interrupting your…ah…meeting, Mr. Wilde." Elliot's face had gone beet red. He stared so intently at the floor that Ryan half expected it to open up and swallow him whole. "But there's an urgent phone call for Ms. Holly."

Evangeline grew deadly still. "Do you know who it is? It's not about my grandfather, is it?"

Ryan shot to his feet. *No, damn it. Please no.*

Elliot shook his head. "It's your landlord."

Chapter Eleven

As if Evangeline's life hadn't already become enough of a train wreck, she was now officially homeless. At least that's what the scary-looking eviction notice posted on her door implied.

Her landlord hadn't minced words when she'd picked up the phone at the Bennington. *No dogs.* That was it. That's all he'd said, then he'd slammed the phone down. Hard.

She hadn't known what to do, and at first she'd been more concerned about Olive's and Bee's safety than the pesky detail of where she'd sleep at night. What if her landlord had called animal control and reported them? What if they were sitting in a cement cell at the pound? What if they'd been separated?

In her panic, she hadn't objected when Ryan insisted on accompanying her to her building to see just how bad the situation was. She'd been grateful for Tony and the limo, otherwise she never would have made it home so quickly. She'd been grateful for Ryan's presence, too. For some reason she felt like things couldn't come completely apart while he was there, even though she had a sneaky suspicion he simply didn't want to let her out of his sight in case she fled.

Her fault, obviously.

She should have done something with that letter of resignation when she realized what a mistake it had been. She should have buried it in the depths of her handbag. Or shredded it. Better yet, she should never have written it in the first place.

But she couldn't think about that right now. Because even though Olive and Bee were completely fine, snug in their dog bed, right where she'd left them, there was a horrible red sign on the door of her apartment. It said Notice to Vacate in a font large enough to be read from space, because Evangeline hadn't already experienced enough humiliation in recent months.

Once satisfied that the dogs were indeed safe and sound, she went back outside to square off with her landlord, who was busy pacing back and forth on the narrow sidewalk in front of the building. It would have been nice if he'd shoveled it while he was out there, but she refrained from making that suggestion.

"Please, Mr. Burton," she said, just shy of begging. "I just need a few days to figure something out, to find a new apartment. A week, maybe?"

What was she saying? She'd never be able to find an affordable, pet-friendly building with a move-in

date in less than seven days. She'd been combing the
real estate ads since the day she'd brought Olive and
Bee home and hadn't found a thing she could afford.
If she had, she wouldn't be standing on the snowy
sidewalk arguing with her landlord while her boss/
erstwhile lover and his chauffeur looked on.

She'd asked Ryan to leave, but so far, he'd stayed
put. She didn't bother getting angry. He'd had a front-
row seat to all of her recent humiliations. Why should
this one be any different?

"This is a no-pets building. You knew that when
you signed the lease." Mr. Burton, who'd never had
a particularly friendly demeanor to begin with,
frowned beneath his supersized mustache.

"I did. But the dogs are my grandfather's, and they
had nowhere else to go. They're very well behaved.
Just one more week? Two?"

"You can stay, but those dogs can't. No way." He
shook his head. "I want those filthy animals out of
here. If I let you keep the dogs, everyone will want
to have dogs. This is an apartment building, not an
animal shelter."

Ryan shot the man a murderous look and came to
stand at her side. "There's no reason to be so harsh.
Surely we can all work something out."

Her landlord looked Ryan up and down, and then
he glanced briefly at the limo and rolled his eyes.
"You can't buy her way out of this. She broke the
rules."

Evangeline cut her gaze toward Ryan. "It's fine.
I'm handling it."

She took a deep breath and faced Mr. Burton
again. "Five days. Surely you can give me that long."

He shook his head. "Zero days, unless you get rid of the mutts."

Mutts? She gasped. "You did *not* just call them that."

Ryan reached for her hand and gave it a squeeze. "Come on, love. Let's take Olive and Bee and go. You don't want to stay here anymore."

He was right. She didn't. But where was she supposed to go with two elderly, special-needs dogs?

She shook her head. "I just can't believe you're throwing me out with no notice whatsoever. Is this even legal?"

Mr. Burton shrugged. "I'm not throwing you out. I'm throwing those dogs out. Get rid of them, and you can stay. They're not yours, anyway. You just said so. If that's true, send them to stay with your mom and dad. Your sister. Anyone. They just can't stay here."

She flinched as if she'd been slapped. "For your information, I don't have a mom and dad. *Or* a sister."

"We're finished here." Ryan's arm came down between her and Mr. Burton, then before she could object, he pulled her close to his side and began steering her toward the car.

She couldn't believe this was happening, but she should have seen it coming. She had, after all, broken the rules.

Still, it would have been nice if she'd been evicted before she found out she was pregnant. She already had serious doubts about her mothering instincts, and this wasn't exactly inspiring confidence in her ability to properly care for a helpless baby.

"Sit." Ryan pointed at the buttery leather seat in

the back of the limousine. The look on his face told her arguing wasn't an option.

Besides, she didn't have much fight left in her after squaring off with her landlord. His suggestion to send Olive and Bee to live with her parents had caught her off guard, stripping her of every last shred of confidence.

The truth was, sometimes she forgot just how alone she really was. Sometimes she was too busy trying to forge ahead, preparing for the sommelier exam or thinking about what wine she'd suggest to Carlo Bocci if she ever actually had the chance to serve him, live and in the flesh. Sometimes she very purposefully didn't allow herself to think about what the future would look like once her grandfather died and once Olive and Bee were gone, and she had no one left.

Sometimes she was simply distracted from her loneliness by the devastatingly gorgeous man who'd fallen into her lap and didn't seem to have any plans to go anywhere, no matter how convinced she was that he'd eventually break her heart.

And here he was. Again.

Somehow, some way, even though she was homeless, and even though she didn't have the first clue how to be a mother and she was probably going to get fired for fleeing her workplace two days in a row, she didn't feel so alone anymore.

Maybe this was what hope felt like.

"Give me your keys," Ryan said.

She dropped them into his outstretched hand.

"Wait here. I'm getting the dogs." A vein throbbed in his left temple. His gaze shot toward Tony, giving

Evangeline a perfect view of the fascinating, angry knot that had formed in his jaw. "Make sure that jerk leaves her alone while I'm gone. Got it?"

Adrenaline trickled through her veins.

Tony nodded. "Yes, Mr. Wilde."

It wasn't adrenaline. It was something more… pleasant. She squirmed in her seat. Was she seriously feeling aroused at a time like this?

Impossible.

She called after him. "Ryan?"

He turned. The resolve in his gaze sent a shiver coursing through her.

Not so impossible, after all.

She swallowed. "Can you get the bottle of wine, too? The one in the wine cabinet in the living room?"

She couldn't leave it there. That wine was special. One of a kind. It would have been easier to go get it herself, but she didn't dare move. Not when Ryan had suddenly gone into alpha male–protector mode.

He gave her a curt nod and stalked back toward her building.

While he was gone, she concentrated on getting her skittering heartbeat under control. And reminding herself that she was an independent woman who didn't need rescuing. Except it felt good to let someone take control, for once. She'd been on her own for so long, she'd forgotten what it felt like to be cared for. Protected. Jeremy had never stood up for her as Ryan just had. In all fairness, she'd never given him the chance. She hadn't wanted to.

Moments later, Ryan emerged, holding the bottle of red in one hand and two dog leashes in the other. Olive and Bee trotted merrily out in front of him.

They were obviously on doggy autopilot because they tried to drag him in the direction of the dog park, but he made a few adorable cooing sounds and they immediately turned around, ready to follow him off into the sunset.

Evangeline's heart gave a wistful little tug. She averted her gaze, but not before her eyes went misty.

She blamed pregnancy hormones. And the frosty winter air. Because she absolutely couldn't be getting emotional at the sight of Ryan Wilde walking her dogs.

A tear slid down her cheek.

Too late.

He exchanged a few words with Tony, who helped the dogs into the limo, and then slid in beside her with the bottle of wine tucked neatly under his arm. Bee immediately scurried into Evangeline's lap. Olive settled on the back seat between them.

"Thank you," she said as the car pulled away from the curb.

"You're welcome," he said quietly.

He was saying and doing all the right things, but now that they were alone again, he couldn't seem to look her in the eye anymore. It hurt. More than she wanted to admit.

His words from earlier kept echoing in her mind, on constant repeat.

Do you have any idea how finding a letter like that would have felt?

She'd messed up. He was probably counting the seconds until they got back to the Bennington and he could put her and her troublesome dogs into a hotel room and walk away from this mess.

"Once we get back to the hotel, I'll figure something out," she said. There had to be somewhere she could go. New York City had more Realtors than the rest of the country combined. She'd find something. She had to.

But then the limo turned right when it should have turned left. Evangeline could see the snow-tipped trees of Central Park on the horizon when Grand Central Station should have been coming into view instead.

She swiveled toward Ryan. "Wait a minute. This isn't the direction of the Bennington."

"No, it's not," he said evenly.

He smoothed down his tie, which now had a large puddle of dog drool in the center of its woven silk pattern. Ryan didn't seem to notice. Either that, or he didn't care.

Evangeline blinked furiously again. *Do not cry. He's probably got an entire walk-in closet full of Hermès. The fact that he's letting your half-blind dog drool all over one necktie doesn't mean anything.*

She cleared her throat. "Are we taking some secret alternate route back to the hotel?"

It was possible. Tony was a miracle worker. He clearly knew Manhattan like the back of his hand.

But somehow she doubted it. Ryan was too quiet. His eyes were too steely, the set of his jaw too tense.

"No, Evangeline." Olive crawled into Ryan's lap. He rested a hand on her back, but his gaze remained glued on the scenery out the window, whizzing past them in a crystalline blur of white. "I'm taking you home."

* * *

"This really isn't necessary." Evangeline stood in the center of Ryan's living room, looking far too much like she belonged there, and crossed her arms. "I mean, thank you. I appreciate it more than I can say. But it's a huge imposition."

Bee shuffled into view from the direction of Ryan's bedroom with Olive hot on her heels. Each dog had one of his shoes dangling from their destructive little mouths. The shoes weren't a matching set, either, ensuring maximum damage.

"It's not an imposition at all," he lied. Somehow he managed to keep a straight face.

What was he supposed to do? Watch and do nothing while the mother of his child got tossed onto the street? Over his dead body.

"I'm sure if I called Elliot and explained the situation he'd find a room at the Bennington we could use for a day or two." She bit her lip, not looking entirely sure.

Ryan knew calling Elliot would be her absolute last resort. Evangeline didn't believe in mixing business with her personal life, a fact Ryan knew all too well. "Think again. Elliot is severely allergic to pet dander. I don't think you'll get much sympathy from him."

She blinked. "How do you even know that?"

"A certain former US president spent two nights in the Bennington penthouse with a certain pair of Portuguese water dogs last year, and Elliot sneezed for three straight weeks afterward."

She let out a snort of laughter. "Are you making that up?"

Some of the tension in Ryan's muscles loosened slightly. For the first time since their near kiss in his office earlier he fully met her gaze. "No, it's true."

She smiled at him, and it seemed to blossom from somewhere deep inside. That thing about pregnant women glowing? He'd never believed it before. Until now.

"I thought Portuguese water dogs were supposed to be hypoallergenic," she said.

"Not for extreme allergy sufferers, apparently."

"Like Elliot?"

Ryan nodded.

Were they really going to stand there and discuss their coworker's dog allergy instead of talking about what was—or *wasn't*—going on between them? He sighed. "I haven't kidnapped you, Evangeline. You're free to go."

Olive or Bee—Ryan wasn't sure which—made a snuffling noise. Then, as if to prove a point, the furry nonhostages abandoned their stolen shoes and curled into a contented pile by the fireplace.

Evangeline's glow dimmed, ever so slightly. "I never said you'd kidnapped me."

No, but you're already planning your escape.

"It's only temporary, though. Until I find something else." She nodded resolutely. "Obviously."

"Obviously," he echoed.

What were they doing?

They were having a baby together, and they couldn't even manage to have an honest conversation about their feelings.

She looked up at him, and he could see his own

doubts swirling in her sapphire eyes. They were both in over their heads, drowning in all the words they couldn't say…desires they couldn't quite contain. And like most drowning victims, they were flailing, lashing out, when in reality, they just might be destined to save one another.

"I was never going to just leave that letter in your chair, Ryan. I want you to know that." Her lips curved into a sad smile.

In another time, another place, he'd kissed those lips. He'd tasted them, worshipped them. When the time was right, he would again. "Do you really want to resign?"

He wanted to be supportive. He wanted to tell her it was okay if she still wanted to quit. But it wasn't okay, damn it. The Bennington needed her.

He needed her.

"What is it that you want, Evangeline?"

Tell me.

Say it.

Her gaze flicked toward his bedroom and then back to him. She exhaled a shaky breath. "I don't want to resign."

It wasn't everything he wanted to hear, but it was enough. For now. "Promise me you'll stay until Bocci shows up."

She nodded, then frowned. "What if he never comes?"

"He will." He'd better. "He's in New York until the end of the month. Just give it until then."

And then what?

He didn't know. He was just trying to buy some time—time to convince her to stay.

"Okay, I promise." Her lips parted, as though she wanted to say something more.

He waited, but then she grew quiet again.

He narrowed his gaze. "Tell me something?"

She nodded. "Anything."

He'd let her ask the questions before. It was only fair that the tables were turned.

"What happened to your mom and dad?" He'd seen the pain in her eyes when her jerk landlord suggested she pawn Olive and Bee off on her parents. There was a story there.

She grew very still for a moment, then took a deep breath. "I don't know, actually. I haven't seen either one of them in years. My mom left when I was nine years old. Afterward, everything just fell apart. My father couldn't cope. He stopped hosting tours at the family winery, stopped harvesting the grapes. The vineyard crumbled around us."

And what about her? Had her father stopped taking care of Evangeline, too?

Ryan didn't have to ask. The answer was in her eyes. It was in the door she'd slammed in his face, not just once, but twice. It was in her stubborn reluctance to let him help her, even when she needed it most.

"My grandfather didn't realize how bad things were until my dad lost the winery. He saved me, but he was too late to save the vineyard. I went to live with him. It was supposed to be temporary, but my dad just kind of drifted away and never came back for me." She squared her shoulders and drew herself more upright, defiant in the face of rejection.

"That's why you and your grandfather are so close." Ryan nodded. "I understand. I went through something similar."

She blinked. "You did?"

"Yes, my parents were both addicts. They weren't ready for the responsibility of a kid, so my aunt and uncle took me in."

"Zander's family?" A lock of Evangeline's hair fell from her messy bun, a casualty of her tumultuous day. It was the only outward sign that anything was amiss.

He reached and tucked it behind her ear, somehow resisting the urge to let his fingertips linger on the elegant curve of her shoulder. "Yes. My uncle died a few years back, but he was like a father to me. Emily Wilde still treats me as one of her own."

She nodded, and a shiver coursed through her at his touch. "Then I guess you really do understand."

She had walls. They both did. But every so often, when they lifted their gazes skyward at the same time, they caught a glimpse of pure blue heaven. In each other.

What would it be like once those walls finally came tumbling down?

Ryan shoved his hands in his trouser pockets to stop himself from touching her again. Cleared his throat. "Tell me about the wine you asked me to bring with Olive and Bee."

"It's from the family vineyard. The last remaining bottle. As far as I know, anyway." She lit up like she always did when she talked about wine. "It's a caber-net franc. Bold, richly bodied, with notes of tart red cherries and brambly raspberries mixed with warm toast and cedar."

She made it sound so nostalgic. So cozy.

Like home.

"It's the perfect wine to pair with food. I defy you to show me a meal that it wouldn't complement." This was the woman he'd fallen for that night, the one who'd drawn him out of his self-imposed exile. Smart, bold...so full of life.

Utterly captivating.

This side of her couldn't be hidden away, no mat-ter how hard Evangeline tried. Because she was real...as authentic as the little girl who'd been for-gotten by her father. She just didn't know it. If any-one understood that warped sense of self, Ryan did.

"I wouldn't dare." He smiled.

She reached for the bottle, turned it over in her hands and ran the pad of her thumb reverently over the label. "It's also star bright, which is rare for a deep red wine. Almost impossible, actually."

"What does *star bright* mean, exactly?" He was still languishing in the ranks of the pinot grigio drinkers, clueless.

"It's a measure of the wine's clarity, its ability to absorb and reflect light. A wine that's star bright is vivid and luminous, but not quite clear. It has light running through its darkness, like a sparkling rib-bon. It glows." She paused, searching his face. "Does that make sense?"

He let his gaze travel from her sparkling blue eyes

to her cheeks—soft and pink, like rose petals. Her mouth beckoned to him. Ruby red.

She was beautiful. She'd always been beautiful, but now she was more. Now she was radiant. Star bright.

"It makes perfect sense," he said.

Then he bade her good-night while he still could, and went to bed.

Alone.

Chapter Twelve

Hours later, Evangeline lay awake in Ryan's spacious spare bedroom with Olive and Bee nestled at her feet.

His apartment was nothing like she'd imagined it would be. Granted, he lived in a penthouse. Because of course he did. But it was hardly the sleek bachelor pad she'd envisioned. Ryan occupied the top floor of a prewar limestone building in the nine hundredth block of Fifth Avenue. Instead of chrome and black leather, the rooms were filled with rich velvets and elegantly weathered pieces that gave the space a comforting feel.

The French doors in the living room overlooked a terrace with a view of the boathouse in Central Park. Before Evangeline had gone to bed, she'd stood with her hand pressed to the glass, watching skaters twirl across the frozen pond. Come springtime, the ice would thaw and people would race tiny wind-driven sailboats on the water. It was one of the best spots in the city for children. For families.

Under the covers, Evangeline's hands slid over her nightgown and splayed on her stomach. She was only in her first trimester, but already she could feel her body changing—growing rounder, softer. It was a potent reminder that the life she and Ryan had created was real. They would be a family someday. Someday soon.

Whatever did or didn't happen between them, they'd be bonded together forever.

She'd been so wrong about Ryan. And yet, deep down she'd known he was a good man. She'd sensed it on that morning so many weeks ago when he'd stood there with dog hair clinging to his Armani jacket while he tried to convince her to see him again. Otherwise, he wouldn't have frightened her so.

She'd had reason to be afraid. Ryan was everything she wanted, everything she needed. Just the kind of man who could break her heart.

But something about lying there in the dark with her head on his pillows and his child growing inside her made her bold. Fearless. Ryan was right next door, and they weren't at the Bennington anymore. There were alone—in his home. And he'd brought her here. He could have taken her anywhere, but he'd brought her home.

What would happen if she went to him now? What would happen if she tiptoed into his room and slid into bed beside him?

The thought was intoxicating. It sent liquid warmth

skittering through her body, like she'd just sipped from a glass of rich Spanish sherry.

What is it that you want, Evangeline?

He'd given her a chance, and she'd blown it.

You. I want you.

The words had been right there, on the tip of her tongue. They tasted as wild and sweet as sun-ripened grapes plucked straight from the vine. But she hadn't been able to say them, hadn't been brave enough to give voice to her desire. Because this time was different. This time, it would be more than just physical. She could lie to herself all she wanted, but no amount of denial would change the fact that she had feelings for Ryan. She just wasn't altogether sure what those feelings were.

He's the father of your baby.

Maybe this need to touch him—this need to feel his hard flesh beneath her fingertips and his mouth, hot and needy, against hers—was biological. Maybe it was primal, her body crying out for more of him.

Or maybe it was just fate.

Either way, she was tired of trying to fight it. So very tired. She slipped out of bed as quietly as possible so as not to disturb Olive and Bee. Then she closed the door behind her and made her way to Ryan's room. The door was closed. She considered knocking, then thought better of it. She didn't want him to turn her away. Not again. Not this time.

Her hand was steady as she turned the doorknob, and that's when she knew she was sure. No hesitation. No doubt. No regrets.

Moonlight streamed through the bedroom windows, casting shadows of gently falling snow over the massive bed in the center of the room. The bed sheets took on a lavender hue in the darkness, and Evangeline felt as if she were entering some strangely beautiful winter wonderland, a frosted fairy tale.

But this was no fairy tale, and the man whose lean body was stretched out before her, all hard planes and sculpted flesh, was very much real. He gazed up at her, his eyes glittering in the shadows. If he was surprised to find her sneaking into his bedroom in the middle of the night, he hid it well. He looked more as if he'd been lying there, waiting for her. As if he'd summoned her with the pure intensity of his desire.

"Evangeline." His voice scraped her insides, making her heart beat hard and fast.

She leaned down, letting her hair fall against his cheek and whispered, "Call me Eve." She swallowed. "Please."

He nodded, cupped her face in his hands then slid his fingertips into her hair. His hands curled into gentle fists, and she could feel the tension in his body, flowing from him to her. Days…weeks…of wanting one another, of desire, of denial.

No more.

No more denial. No more waiting.

"Let me see you, Eve," he growled.

She rested a hand on his chest and straightened, savoring his gaze on her as she gathered the hem of her nightgown in her hands and lifted it slowly over her head. His gaze raked over her bare body, and she felt it as keenly as a caress, traveling down her neck, over her collarbone and then lingering on her breasts. A delicious warmth pooled low in her center, and even though she'd undressed for him before, she had the unmistakable feeling that she was being seen for the very first time. Truly seen, body and soul.

When his gaze moved to her newly rounded belly, a smile tipped his lips and his eyes grew shiny in the darkness. "Mine."

His.

He was talking about the baby, not her. But for a minute, she let herself pretend he wasn't. She closed her eyes and let the word wash over her, bathing her in love and light.

Ryan's hands found hers, and he pulled her toward him until she straddled his body on the bed. When she opened her eyes, he looked at her with such adoration, such reverence that she thought maybe, just maybe, he'd been talking about her, after all.

Mine.

His.

He rested his fingertips gently on her stomach. "Ours."

She smiled down at him. "Kiss me, Ryan."

He rose up, captured her chin in his grasp and in the torturous moment before his lips touched hers, he murmured. "Oh, baby, I thought you'd never ask."

Evangeline's breath caught in her throat. The kiss was slow and gentle. Achingly tender. She fought back tears as she opened for him and his tongue slid languidly against hers. Every movement, every taste was delicately drawn out. The sweetness of it caught her off guard.

She'd been prepared for heat—for a shuddering, frenzied end to the attraction that had been swirling between them for so long. But this was no frantic coupling. They weren't just looking for a release.

They were seeking something else, and as much as Evangeline wanted it, *needed* it, she was terrified of what it meant.

This isn't sex, she thought as she let her hands roam his chest and abdomen, exploring every tantalizing dip, every ridge of muscle. *This...this...is making love*.

Still, beneath the tenderness—beneath the feather-soft kisses and the broken sighs—an excruciating need burned deep inside. Evangeline's nerve endings felt like they were on fire. His erection pressed against her center, thick and hard. She ground against him, whimpering.

"I'm here," he whispered against her lips. "Right here."

Then his mouth dropped to her nipple and the whimper turned into a low, sultry moan. It was a sound she'd never heard herself make before, and in a strange, sublime way it made sense because this body was new to her. It was changing every day, blossoming into something wonderfully different. Her breasts had grown fuller, sensitive to the barest touch. When he moved to the other nipple and drew it into his mouth, sucking gently, she nearly came apart.

"Please," she breathed, and she wasn't sure what all she was begging for.

She wanted him inside her. Now. She wanted to feel his hardness pushing into her until they became one, but she wanted more than that. She wanted all of him—all of this beautiful, broken man who made her believe she could have a life she'd never dared to imagine.

A future.

A family.

So she reached for him, reveling in the way his breath caught when her fingers wrapped around his erection. Then she guided him to her entrance and lowered herself over him, taking him in. He rose up to kiss her as their bodies came together, and at first there was nothing but an overwhelming, exquisite sense of relief. Like she could finally breathe again after a long, lonely season underwater.

But all at once the heat began to build. He curled his strong hands around her hips and thrust into her. Harder. And harder, until she felt like a shimmering, heavenly thing—a brilliant, beautiful fire. More light than dark. A flame in the night.

Star bright.

It felt like a fever dream. Too colorful, too vibrant to be real.

But Ryan knew it couldn't be a figment of his imagination, because as long as he'd waited for this night, as much as he'd wanted it, the reality of making love to Evangeline was infinitely sweeter than any fantasy he could have conjured.

She looked so beautiful rising and falling above him with her hair tumbling over her shoulders and spilling over her bare breasts. He remembered everything about their previous night together, every supple curve of her body. But she'd changed in the weeks since they'd been together. There was a new softness to her—and it was more than the pregnancy, more than merely physical.

She was more open to him now, more vulnerable. When he rolled her over so that she was beneath him and then gathered her wrists in one hand, pinning them over her head, she purred like a kitten. The sound was nearly enough to bring him to climax right then and there, but he clenched his jaw and fought the release. This night had been months in the making. He wanted, *needed*, to make it last.

For her.

For *them*.

He slid from her body, murmuring wicked promises at her whimper of protest. Poised over her, he moved down the lovely, writhing length of her, pausing to take a nipple into his mouth again. She arched toward him, crying his name as his hands found the tender insides of her thighs and guided them apart.

His mouth moved lower, and she opened her eyes, questions glittering in her gaze.

"Trust me," he whispered, smiling at the knowledge that this was new for her, that even after making a baby together he could show her a new kind of intimacy. A gift for them both.

He pressed an openmouthed kiss to her belly, then dipped his head even lower, giving her the most intimate kiss of all. She gasped at the first touch of his tongue. Then he circled her slowly, gently with the pad of his thumb as he licked his way inside. She shivered against his mouth, and her hips rose up off the bed. He slid his hand beneath her perfect bottom, holding her still.

She was close. So close.

Her hands were tangled in his hair, and her breath was coming hard and fast. He could taste the honeyed prelude to her release, so decadently sweet. He stopped, moved over her once again and braced his hands on either side of her head.

Her face was deliciously flushed, her eyes were closed and her lips bee-stung, swollen from his kisses. Ryan had never seen anyone so radiant. Lost in pleasure, lost in love.

His erection throbbed at her opening.

Love.

Is that what this was?

How would he know? He knew nothing of love, nothing of commitment or what it took to build a home—a real home where the walls rang with laughter and where people took care of each other. Where they *stayed.*

But when Evangeline's lashes fluttered open and she looked at him through heavy-lidded eyes, he almost believed he could.

"Just you and me." He pushed inside her again.

He'd made her a promise, and he'd honored it. There were no ghosts in this bed. This was about them, and only them. Except they weren't a couple anymore. They were a family...almost. "Just *us.*"

Then she shattered around him for a second time, and he couldn't hold back any longer. He thrust into her and came with a deep, shuddering groan that felt like it had been ripped straight from his soul.

For a prolonged moment, neither of them moved.

He squeezed his eyes closed tight, savoring the sound of their intermingled breath and the snow falling lightly against the windows. New York... Bennington 8...the Michelin star...all of it felt so far away. So long as he was inside her, nothing else could touch them. Nothing could tear them apart.

"Ryan."

He opened his eyes. Evangeline gazed up at him, her sapphire irises shining bright with unshed tears.

"What if I'm just like her?" she whispered. "What if I'm just like my mother?"

"Oh, baby, you're not." He shifted, and pulled her close, tucking her head beneath his chin. Her panicked heartbeat crashed against his, and he wrapped his arms around her as tightly as he could.

She'd undressed for him. Not just in body, but also in soul. He knew without having to ask that she was sharing her deepest fear—the thing standing between them, threatening to pull them apart. Even here, even now.

"How do you know?" she said into his chest.

He wondered if she could hear his heart breaking in that moment—breaking for her. Evangeline Holly, the woman who cared more about a pair of blind and deaf dogs than where she slept at night, was afraid she'd follow in her mother's footsteps and abandon her own child.

"Because I do." He swallowed. *I do.* Wedding words. "Look at me, Eve."

He captured her chin and tipped her face upward, so she met his gaze. "I never knew your mother, but I know you. You have more love and devotion in your heart than anyone I've ever known. I see it. I see *you.* Even when you're trying to push me away, I see you. Our baby couldn't ask for a better mother."

She gave him a wobbly smile. "Our baby."

"Yes, ours. Yours and mine."

She closed her eyes and burrowed into him, and while his chest was still wet with her tears, she fell into a deep sleep. And still he held her, whispering reassurances into her silky hair, hoping they would somehow take root. She didn't have to do this alone. He'd be there, too. Neither of them had had a perfect childhood, but that didn't matter. They were two broken people, but together they were whole. So long as they helped each other, just like Olive and Bee, everything would be all right.

More than all right. It would be perfect…

If only she believed.

He wasn't sure how long they stayed that way, wrapped around one another, before he finally drifted off. But sometime before dawn, after the heavy snow had lightened to delicate flurries that coated the city in a fine layer of sugar, a shot of arousal dragged him back to consciousness. When he opened his eyes, Evangeline was moving over him, taking him in again. He groaned, reaching to cup her full breasts, running his thumbs over their soft pink peaks.

She leaned forward to kiss him, and her hair fell around them in a shimmering gold curtain, sheltering them from the outside world. It was slow this time, gentle and easy.

Easier than it should have been in a room swollen with doubts.

Chapter Thirteen

Ryan didn't know if Evangeline would come to him again the following night, or if she'd considered their most recent coupling another one-time thing. A moment of weakness.

The relief that coursed through him when she entered his bedroom, undressed, with her hair gathered in loose waves over one shoulder, was frightening in its intensity. It wasn't until she'd slipped into his bed for five nights in a row that he let himself come to expect it. On the sixth night, they didn't even go through the pretense of retiring to separate bedrooms. Olive and Bee claimed the guest bed as their own, and Ryan led Evangeline to his bed by the hand. Her lips tipped into a bashful smile as he undressed her and as always, he marveled at the sight of her ever-changing body. So beautiful in its purpose.

But their trysts were always ushered in by the violet hour and ended when the sun came up. They never spoke of the change in their relationship. At work, everything remained the same.

Which was fine.

For now.

Evangeline had promised to stay until Carlo Bocci made an appearance at Bennington 8, but the month would eventually come to a close. Until then, Ryan was certain of only two things—he wasn't ready to give Evangeline up, and he couldn't keep lying to Zander. It was time to confess.

The events of the past few days couldn't have gone unnoticed. Ryan and Evangeline had bolted out of the building without providing any sort of explanation. Twice. And then there'd been the near kiss in his office, witnessed by dog-averse Elliot. Ryan had some explaining to do, and it seemed like a good idea to do it before Zander grew impatient and decided to fire them both.

Not that Zander could actually fire Ryan. He owned shares in the Bennington. Ryan served on the board of directors. They were family, and they'd always operated as a team. As CEO, Zander had never pulled rank on Ryan before.

Then again, Ryan had never even considered dating a hotel employee, much less moving in with one of them. And having a baby.

Damn.

It sounded bad. Really bad. How had he let things get so out of hand without talking to Zander? His cousin had every right to be pissed. The triple espresso Ryan had waiting on his desk as a peace offering first thing Thursday morning seemed wholly inadequate.

Zander's gaze snagged on it the moment he crossed the threshold. He stared at the coffee, then slowly switched his attention to Ryan, sitting in one of the wingback chairs opposite his desk.

"A triple." He arched a brow. "Things must be dire."

"Not dire," Ryan said. *Just...big.* "But I did give some thought to adding a shot of whiskey."

"At seven in the morning? I'll pass." Zander set down his briefcase and downed half the espresso in a swift gulp.

He sat and leaned back in his chair. His posture may have been casual, but his stare was pure intensity. Pure Zander. "I suppose you're here to tell me you're sleeping with our wine director."

If only it were that simple.

Ryan released a breath. "How long have you known?"

"I suspected as much the day she turned up for her interview. There's no mistaking the way you look at her. I've known you my entire life, remember? I haven't seen you look at a woman like that since—" Zander paused to reconsider "—ever, actually."

"Evangeline and I met before the interview," Ryan admitted.

Zander's eyebrows rose. "When?"

"A couple of months ago. I didn't expect to see her again, and then she showed up here. It was a nice surprise." An understatement, obviously. He was going to have to be more forthcoming, but he also wanted to respect Evangeline's privacy. Zander didn't need a play-by-play of their entire relationship.

So now it's an actual relationship?

He cleared his throat. "There's more."

Zander nodded. "I suspected as much."

"She's pregnant."

Zander grinned, but didn't seem the least bit surprised. "I wondered when you were going to get around to telling me."

Ryan shifted in his chair. "You knew that, too?"

Clearly he and Evangeline hadn't been as successful as they'd hoped at keeping things under wraps.

Zander let out a wry laugh. "I figured it out around the time you doused her in Côtes du Rhône. It wasn't the subtlest of moves."

Touché.

"Plus Allegra had an interesting conversation with your Miss Holly a few days ago. She had a feeling you two had some news to share."

Ryan nodded.

My Miss Holly.

She wasn't his. Not yet, anyway.

He cleared his throat. "Things between Evangeline and me are…complicated. Neither of us were expecting this."

"But is it what you want? That's the real question, isn't it?" Zander leaned forward. "I never expected Allegra to come back into my life. I wasn't ready, and neither was she. She was probably *less* ready. But deep down, it's what we wanted. Ready or not."

Zander made it sound so simple, but Ryan had been there. He'd seen the way Zander fought for

Allegra. And now here they were, months later…
married and happy.

A wistful ache churned in Ryan's gut. He didn't
realize he'd grown quiet until Zander broke the
loaded silence by opening and closing one of his
desk drawers.

When Ryan looked up, he found Zander watching
him with an expression he hadn't seen on his cousin's
face since they were kids growing up together in the
Wilde family brownstone. He'd dropped his CEO
aura and was giving off a distinct big brother vibe.

"Look, cousin. There's no easy way for me to do
this, so I'm just going to come out and say it." Zander took a deep breath. "Evangeline is great and if
you two end up together, no one will be happier for
you than I will. I promise you that. But I've been
worried about you for a long time now. The whole
family has."

The ache in Ryan's gut sharpened. Zander was
going to bring up Natalie. He probably should have
seen it coming. Maybe on some level, he had. Maybe
that's why he'd waited so long to tell him what was
going on.

"You don't need to worry about me. I'm fine," he
said through gritted teeth.

"I know." Zander's gaze dropped to his desk. "But
after what happened with Natalie, I also know you
want to be sure."

A trickle of alarm snaked down Ryan's spine as
Zander bent to retrieve something from the opened
drawer and set it on the surface of the desk between
them. It was a flat white box with some sort of labo-
ratory symbol on the side. Zander pushed it toward

him, and he got a better look at the block lettering in
the upper right-hand corner of the cardboard.

Noninvasive Prenatal Paternity Test.

Ryan glared at Zander. "What the hell is that?"

"A paternity test. You just said yourself that your
relationship with Evangeline is complicated. You
barely know one another."

"I know enough," Ryan said quietly.

Did believing Evangeline make him a fool? Perhaps. Zander apparently thought so.

"I care about you, man. You were a mess after
Natalie's baby was born. I just don't want to see you
go through that again."

"I won't," he snapped. His mood was suddenly
black enough for a fight. He and Zander hadn't come
to blows since they were twelve years old, but something about seeing that box on the table made his
hands curl into fists.

Zander held up his hands. "I'll drop it. It's your
call. Just do me a favor and take the kit in case you
change your mind."

Ryan took the box and slipped it into his pocket,
out of sight. Looking at it made him feel sick. "Fine.
But for the record, Evangeline is nothing like Natalie. She's…" He was at a sudden loss for words as a
series of images flashed through his consciousness—
Evangeline sabering the top off a champagne bottle; grabbing him by the lapels and hauling him into
her apartment so her neighbor wouldn't spot Olive
and Bee; smiling at him as she reached for him in
the night.

Zander, waiting, lifted a brow.

"She's special," he finally said.

Zander nodded. "She's also important to Bennington 8."

"Yes, I'm aware. She can still do her job, if that's what you're worried about. Quite effectively, I might add." She'd been pouring wine like a pro for six nights running. She knew enough about the various vintages to make recommendations without having to sample bottles. She was ready for Bocci. They all were.

"Exactly. I need to know she's all in," Zander said. *All in.*

"She is. There's nothing to worry about. We've talked about it, and she's assured me she's staying on until Bocci's visit. She knows how important it is. She gave me her word. She's all in."

All in as far as Bennington 8, anyway. As for the rest of it, he wasn't so sure.

Evangeline felt a little faint as she walked into the nursing home with Olive and Bee bobbing gleefully at the ends of their leashes. Pregnancy hormones. Or more likely, nerves. Tonight was her weekly pizza date with Grandpa Bob, and she'd also decided it was the night she was going to tell him about the baby.

She couldn't keep it from him. He meant too much to her. She couldn't lie to him if she tried. Not about something like this.

Being the supportive person he was, she knew he'd be happy for her. But she still wasn't looking forward to the conversation, probably because it wasn't as if she could just drop a bomb like a pregnancy on her elderly grandfather and not expect him to ask about the father.

Oh, didn't I tell you? I broke up with the guy you hated, and now I'm having an affair with my boss.

Her face went hot.

An affair? Is that what it was?

She had no idea. She was still trying to wrap her mind around the fact that she was having a baby. It was hard enough to start thinking of herself as a mother. She couldn't begin to think of herself as someone's wife.

Getting ahead of ourselves, aren't we? Who said anything about marriage?

No one had. Certainly not Evangeline.

Olive and Bee twitched their noses as they trotted past the dining room. The air was already heavy with the scent of pepperoni, and Evangeline held her breath. Just in case. Her body couldn't seem to decide if it was prone to morning sickness or not. One day, she'd feel fine and then two days later the smells coming from the kitchen at Bennington 8 would make her want to hurl. This biological ambivalence certainly didn't improve her confidence in her mothering abilities. Even her body didn't know what it was doing.

When she reached Grandpa Bob's room, he was sitting in front of his television with his back to the door. His hearing wasn't what it used to be, even with his hearing aids, so he didn't turn around. She paused for a moment, swallowing around the lump in her throat.

He looked so frail. She couldn't get used to the sight of the walker sitting beside his recliner or the guardrails that had been installed on either side of the bed that he'd brought with him from his apartment.

Everything in the room was so familiar, but somehow managed to look different. Smaller somehow. Evangeline's grandpa had loomed so large over her life. He'd always been the one reliable presence in a sea of confusion. The dependable one. The strong one. Now they'd switched places, and she was still struggling to live up to the task.

She bent to unclip Olive and Bee from their leashes, and they scurried over to him at once, vying for space in his lap.

He laughed. "Hello there, little ones."

Evangeline settled onto the matching recliner— the same one where she'd curled up and done her homework as a little girl—and waited for the dogs to calm down. After five full minutes of tail wagging and excited yips, they planted themselves on either side of Granda Bob. Within seconds, they were both snoring.

"They miss you," Evangeline said, as her heart gave a little twist. She had zero regrets about the whole eviction thing. None whatsoever.

"I miss them, too, but they certainly seem to be happy." Grandpa Bob let out a laugh. "Not to mention well-fed."

Evangeline cleared her throat. Ryan liked to bring home doggie bags for Olive and Bee from Bennington 8. Last night they'd dined on leg of lamb. "We should probably keep them away from the pizza."

"Easier said than done. I speak from experience," he said.

"I'll guard my slice with my life."

"That might be what it takes." He glanced at the

digital clock on top of the television. "Shall we head on down to the dining room?"

"Can we chat for a minute first? There's something I want to talk to you about." Her tummy gave another nervous flip.

"Sure. Is everything okay?" His brow furrowed.

Spit it out.

"Everything's fine. It's good news, actually. At least I hope you'll think so." She took a deep breath. "I'm pregnant."

For a sliver of a moment, her heart seemed to stall while she waited for his reaction. But then his face split into a wide grin. "Pregnant? Really?"

She nodded. "Yes, really."

"Of course that's good news. It's the best news possible." He beamed. She hadn't seen that kind of light in his eyes in months. Years, maybe. "I'm going to be a great-grandfather."

"And I'm going to be a mom," she said.

"You'll be a wonderful mother, sweetheart. Your baby couldn't ask for a better mom."

"You sound just like Ryan." The words flew out of her mouth before she could stop them. She didn't even realize her mistake until Grandpa Bob's smile faded.

"Who's Ryan?"

"Ryan Wilde." She swallowed. "He's the baby's father."

"So no more what's-his-name, then." Grandpa Bob's eyebrows lifted.

She didn't bother scolding him about pretending to forget Jeremy's name. It was probably time she forgot it herself. "Nope."

"Good. I never liked that guy."

"Yes, I know. You mentioned that a time or two." Why had she never listened? Why had she never believed her grandfather when he'd insisted she deserved better?

Because you never believed it yourself. But you do deserve better.

The words in her head sounded as if they'd been spoken by Ryan, as so many of the thoughts spinning in her consciousness had lately.

Bee stirred, and Grandpa Bob gave the dog a reassuring pat. "Tell me about Ryan. Will I like him?"

"He's wonderful. Olive and Bee are certainly fond of him." *And so am I.* She was afraid to say it out loud, though. Afraid to admit that she might be letting herself fall, when that was the last thing in the world she'd wanted. The risk to her heart was greater now than ever before.

"I trust them. You should, too. They're excellent judges of character." Grandpa Bob winked. "So when's the wedding?"

And there it was.

"There isn't going to be a wedding," she said with a little too much force.

Her adamancy didn't go unnoticed. The light in Grandpa Bob's eyes dimmed, ever so slightly. His expression grew serious. "Ever?"

"Ever." She nodded. Over her grandfather's shoulder, she could see a few of the other residents making their way down the hall toward the dining room. They should probably get down there. Pizza night was really popular around here.

Besides, she was suddenly ready to put an end to this conversation.

"If this Ryan Wilde is so wonderful, why would you say something like that?"

"Because." There was that darned lump in her throat again. *Do* not *cry*. The last thing she wanted was for Grandpa Bob to worry about her, because she was perfectly fine. "It's the twenty-first century. I don't have to get married just because I'm pregnant."

"True." He nodded, but something about the way he looked at her caused the lump in her throat to quadruple in size. "But why do I get the feeling that whatever century we're in has nothing to do with your reluctance to tie the knot?"

"I don't know." She stood, picked up the walker and positioned it closer to his chair. "We're late for dinner. We can talk about this another time."

He glanced at the walker, but didn't budge. "Don't let the choices your parents made rob you of a lifetime of happiness, Evangeline. Your mom and dad both made terrible mistakes. Mistakes that caused you deep pain. No one knows that more than I do."

She shook her head. *No. Please no.* She didn't want to go there. Painful childhood memories had no place at a pizza party.

But Grandpa Bob kept on talking. To make matters worse, Olive and Bee were gazing up at her as though she'd just crushed their dreams of being flower girls. Or in their case, flower dogs. "But it's time to let the past die. You're having a child. That means a new life. A new future. Not just for the baby, but for you, too."

"I know," she whispered.

"Do you? Because I'm not so sure you do. Trust yourself, sweetheart. You'll know love when you see it. It won't look anything like what your parents had. It will look more like sacrifice than selfishness." At last he stood, meeting her gaze head-on. "It'll be like nothing you've ever experienced before. And when it's real, it has a way of repairing old wounds. Believe it."

She smiled a bittersweet smile. "I'll try."

Believe it.

Believe.

Again, the echo in her head sounded so much like Ryan's voice that it was almost as if he was right there.

Whispering in her ear.

Chapter Fourteen

Evangeline stood at the head of one of the larger dining tables in Bennington 8 with six bottles of wine lined up in front of her. Three reds and three whites, arranged from light to dark.

"So to recap, the wines we're featuring this evening are all from France." She glanced at the eight people seated at the table—all of them servers scheduled to work when the restaurant opened in fifteen minutes. Then she pointed at one of them. "Gia, can you name the regions represented by this selection?"

Gia nodded. "The chenin blanc and muscadet are both from the Loire region. We've got a sauvignon blanc and a red blend from Bordeaux, plus two reds from Burgundy—one light and the other bold."

"Excellent. I think we're ready. Any questions before the doors open?" Evangeline gave the group a final once-over, but no one raised a hand. "Very well. I'll be here all night if you need anything. As always, I'll drop by each table personally, but it's important for everyone to have a good understanding of all the wines on offer."

The servers thanked her, and the few that still had wine remaining in their tasting glasses finished it off before leaving to prepare their tables for the evening. Evangeline's glass was still full, of course. But she'd placed it discreetly behind the row of bottles, and no one appeared to notice that she wasn't actually drinking anything.

So far, so good. Her evening wine briefing with the staff had gone exceptionally well, and according to the maître d', Bennington 8 would have a full house tonight. They were booked solid from opening until close.

She'd be on her feet for hours. With any luck, she could escape to Ryan's office for a few minutes of rest before the doors opened. It wasn't until she gathered the bottles and returned them to the wine cooler that she realized he hadn't stopped by her evening tasting like he usually did.

She situated the muscadet back in place, only to realize she'd put the chenin blanc where the Bordeaux was supposed to be. An atypical mistake. But she was feeling a bit…unsettled.

She and Ryan had barely seen one another in the past twenty-four hours. He'd left her a voice mail message while she was at the pizza party letting her know that he'd been called away overnight on business. Something about a hotel property that was about to go on the market in Chicago. He and Zander were thinking about buying it.

She'd been relieved at first. At least that's what she'd told herself. She needed time to shake off the things that Grandpa Bob had said to her. Time to get the ridiculous idea of marriage out of her head. And she couldn't very well do that while she was sleeping in Ryan's bed, with her head on his chest and his hands buried in her hair.

Time to herself would be good.

But then she'd let herself into his apartment, and it had felt so cavernous without him there. So empty. Even Olive and Bee missed him. They'd kept hopping off the sofa during her *Say Yes to the Dress* marathon to scour the penthouse in search of him.

Something's wrong, she thought as she switched the chenin blanc and the Bordeaux. She'd thought he would be back by now. She should have at least heard from him, shouldn't she?

Then again, why should he keep her apprised of his every move? As Grandpa Bob had so bluntly pointed out, she wasn't his wife. She wasn't even his girlfriend. She just happened to be pregnant with his baby.

There's more to it than that, and you know it.

She squared her shoulders, shut the door to the wine cooler and made her way to the maître d' stand. Now wasn't the time to analyze her relationship. Or obsess over why Ryan hadn't contacted her. Or, more disturbingly, why she'd watched six straight episodes of a show that centered around women choosing their wedding dresses. She had less than ten minutes to herself before she began recommending wine for Manhattan's elite.

"If anyone needs me, I'll be in Mr. Wilde's office until we open," she said.

The maitre d' nodded. "Yes, Miss Holly."

His office was empty, which she supposed should be a relief. She wasn't sure how she would have felt if he'd been here all evening and hadn't popped in on her tasting like he usually did. But he'd assured her he'd be back before Bennington 8 opened for dinner. Everyone was on high alert in case Carlo Bocci showed up.

Evangeline doubted he'd come on a Friday night, though. So far all of the restaurant reviews he'd conducted in New York City had been done on weeknights, and Mon Ami Jules was still the only one that had been awarded a Michelin star.

Still, she was starting to worry.

She kicked off her shoes and stretched out on the brandy-colored distressed leather sofa that was situated in the corner of the office, and a chill coursed through her. The snow hadn't let up for days, and it was beginning to look like the city was sleeping beneath a fluffy white down comforter.

She sat up and spied one of Ryan's impeccable suit jackets draped over a hanger on the back of the door. A blanket would have been sublime, but also Armani wool would do nicely.

After sliding the jacket from its hanger, she returned to the sofa and snuggled beneath it in a semi-fetal position. The cool silk lining was soft against her cheek. She closed her eyes and took a deep inhale, filling her senses with his scent—that unique bouquet that was pure romance. Pure Ryan. Oak and pine, with just a hint of sandalwood and crushed wild violets. If he'd been a wine, he'd be a rich, bold red. Her favorite kind.

A second passed, maybe two. If she wasn't careful, she'd fall asleep.

Thank you, first trimester.

She wasn't sure when exactly she gave up the fight or how long she'd been unconscious when a low, familiar voice dragged her from her slumber.

"Hey there, sleeping beauty."

Her eyelashes fluttered open, and she found Ryan bent over her. There were snow flurries in his hair, and laugh lines around his eyes and it was such a surprise, such a *relief*, to see him that the hot sting of tears pressed against the backs of her eyes.

This was bad.

So very bad.

Don't fall in love with him. You can't.

"You're back." She blinked furiously.

"I am." He leaned down and pressed a slow, soft kiss to her lips. His mouth was cold against hers. He tasted of icicles and roasted chestnuts. "Happy to see me?"

More than she wanted to admit, even to herself. "Very."

They'd never kissed in the office before. Never even held hands. This was a first, and it should have scared her, but it didn't. It felt right. "How was your trip?"

"Quite productive." His smile dimmed. "But now I'm worried about you. Are you okay, love?"

"I'm fine. I had a few minutes after the staff tasting, so I thought I'd rest for a bit before we open."

He went quiet for a beat too long, and that's when she noticed the glittering lights of the theater district shining through the office's corner window. The sky was inky black.

"Oh my God." Panic gathered in a tight knot in her chest. She sat up so fast that her head spun a little. "What time is it? How long have I been asleep?"

"It's about eight thirty. Don't worry. I'm sure everything is fine." He brushed the hair back from her face. "Just tell me again that you're feeling all right."

"I am. I promise, but I need to get upstairs. We're booked solid tonight." She'd promised to visit every table personally. Why hadn't anyone come to find her? What was going on up there?

She flew to her feet, and Ryan's jacket—her makeshift blanket—fell to the floor. She'd forgotten all about it. "Oh, sorry."

She bent to pick it up, but he beat her to the punch. "It's okay. I've got it."

He gathered the Armani in his hands, but as he stood back up, something fell from one of its pockets. Evangeline was already hurrying toward the door, and she tripped over it. She stumbled into Ryan, and he caught her by the shoulders so she wouldn't fall.

"Oops, that was a close one." She laughed, but when she pulled back and caught a glimpse of Ryan's face, she knew something was wrong. He'd gone ashen.

"Ryan, what is it?"

"Nothing. It's nothing. Zander…"

She wasn't sure what he said next, because when she followed his gaze to the white box at her feet all she could hear was the sound of her own heartbeat. Impossibly loud, impossibly fast, as if her heart was trying to burst out of her chest.

"Eve, don't," Ryan's voice managed to cut through the fog in her head. "Please."

But it was too late. She'd already bent to pick up the box. She had to. She needed to be sure the letters on the cardboard really spelled out the words she thought she'd read.

They couldn't.

But they did.

Noninvasive Prenatal Paternity Test.

This can't be happening.

Ryan had spent just about every minute he was away thinking about the things he wanted to say to Evangeline upon his return—the promises he wanted to make, the question he wanted to ask her. He'd run through a dozen different scenarios in his head, but not one of them had involved the box that she was currently clutching in her trembling hands.

That godforsaken paternity test.

Damn you, Zander.

A knot of regret wound itself tightly around his throat. He couldn't blame Zander for this disaster. His cousin's motives had been pure. The blame for the wounded look in Evangeline's sapphire eyes rested squarely on his own shoulders. The minute he'd laid eyes on that box, he'd known it was trouble. He should have disposed of it instead of shoving it inside his coat pocket.

But he hadn't. He'd dropped it in the pocket of his Armani as if it was something as inconsequential as a paper clip instead of a hand grenade. And now that grenade had just detonated in the face of the woman he loved.

"Here." She shoved the box at his chest. "You dropped something."

"This isn't what it looks like. I promise it's not." God, he hated himself.

"It looks like a paternity test," she said flatly.

He chucked it in the trash can beside his desk with such force that the wastebasket fell over, rolled across the floor and bumped into the wall. "It's garbage."

She held up a hand. "You don't have to explain, Ryan. I understand. I really do."

But the pain in her gaze told him she didn't. She thought he felt no different about her than he'd felt about Natalie. She thought he didn't trust her. Hell, she probably thought he'd toss her and her sweet little dogs out on the street if the baby she was carrying wasn't his. Why else would he be toting around a paternity test in his pocket?

That wasn't how he felt at all. Not even close. "Understand this, Eve. I'm in love with you."

"No." She shook her head. "You're not."

They were right back to square one. Right back to the morning he'd woken up in her non-pet-friendly apartment in the Village and she'd insisted that he didn't actually want to see her again.

Once more, he was losing her.

"This is all a terrible misunderstanding, and I can explain." She had to believe him. He'd drag Zander into this if he had to. It couldn't be too late.

"I need to go," she said quietly.

She walked past him, and he turned to stop her,

struggling to find the words that would convince her to stay and hear him out. But then she opened the door, and Elliot stood on the other side with his hand poised to knock.

His gaze shot back and forth between them, and he let out an audible sigh of relief. "Thank God you're both here."

"No. Not now." Ryan held up a hand. "Whatever it is, it's going to have to…"

"Carlo Bocci is here," Elliot blurted, cutting him off.

Evangeline froze. *"What?"*

Elliot nodded frantically and tried to elaborate, but his head bobbed up and down faster than he could get the words out. "Yes…he's…"

"Let's calm down," Ryan said, stunned at how calm he managed to sound. "We're ready for this. We've been preparing for weeks."

"You're right. Of course. We're ready." Beads of sweat were breaking out across Elliot's forehead. He looked anything but ready.

Ryan's temples throbbed. Why the hell did this have to happen now? He could barely think straight. All his focus was concentrated on Evangeline and repairing the mess he'd just created. At least Bocci's appearance had kept her there. For the time being, anyway.

Focus. "How long has he been here? Where *exactly* is he?"

Elliot took a deep breath and managed to get himself together long enough to spit out the facts. "He just checked in with the maître d'. He's early. He's got a nine o'clock reservation under a fake name—Mark

Spencer. The maître d' recognized him right away and is planning on seating him at table twenty-five."

"Good." Ryan nodded. Situated in a semiprivate alcove at the right of the entrance, table twenty-five was the best seat in the house. It was spacious and had a sweeping view of the city. They'd been limiting reservations at this particular spot for weeks in anticipation of this exact scenario. "Why hasn't he been seated yet?"

"He asked to visit the bar for a cocktail first." The last remaining splash of color drained from Elliot's face. They hadn't planned on such a request.

Evangeline frowned. "Is that normal?"

"I have no idea," Ryan muttered. "But at least it buys us some time."

"Right." Evangeline took a deep breath. "I've got to go. I need to select his wine."

She was correct, of course—they couldn't keep standing there.

But Ryan was reluctant to let her out of his sight. Actually, that was an understatement. The thought of her walking out the door was killing him.

All in, remember?

He had to trust her. They could finish their discussion later, after Bocci had gone. Everything would be fine. It had to.

"Go." A dull, cavernous pain bloomed in place of his heart.

He implored her with his gaze. *We're not finished here.*

But she turned around and left without casting even a cursory glance in his direction.

"Mr. Wilde." Elliot cleared his throat.

Ryan tore his attention from the empty spot that Evangeline had just vacated and tried to act as if he was on top of things. Totally in control. "Yes?"

"Should I call the other Mr. Wilde and let him know Bocci is here?"

"I'll do it." Zander would want to know what was going on, and Ryan should be the one to fill him in.

Plus, making the call and dealing with Zander would give him something to do. He couldn't pace around Bennington 8 for the duration of Bocci's meal, analyzing every bite the reviewer ate. Nor could he pace the length of his office, waiting to talk to Evangeline. He'd lose his mind.

"Very well," Elliot said. "I'll get back to work."

"Perfect." Someone needed to keep an eye on the rest of the hotel. The night was spinning out of control. Ryan didn't want to contemplate what else could go wrong. "Thank you, Elliot."

The manager gave him a final nod and then left.

Ryan raked a hand through his hair, suddenly exhausted beyond measure. He looked around the office. The overturned trash can and his suit jacket, forgotten in a heap on the floor, were the only outward signs of the chaos that had just taken place. He'd expected worse. It felt like a tornado had just ripped through his life. Shouldn't the paint be peeling off the walls or the building be crumbling down around him?

He righted the trash can, and bile rose to the back of his throat when he caught a glimpse of the paternity test lying at the bottom of the bin. He swallowed it down, picked his jacket up off the floor and hung it back on the hanger where it belonged. Small things, but it helped him feel like he had some semblance of control over his world.

But his life no longer revolved around the Bennington. Not the way it used to. Evangeline was his world now. He wasn't sure when exactly it happened. But it had. At some point during the past two months, everything had shifted. Everything had slipped so perfectly into place—his mind, his heart, his very existence.

For the first time in his life, he was happy.

He was head over heels in love, and he was going to be a father. He didn't need a paternity test to tell him what he already knew. The irony of the whole thing was that he would have loved Evangeline and her baby, regardless of genetics. They belonged together.

Now he could only hope that once this surreal night was over, Evangeline would listen.

He took a ragged inhale, pulled his cell phone from his pocket and dialed Zander. His cousin answered on the third ring.

Ryan didn't mince words. "Carlo Bocci is here. He's got a nine o'clock reservation."

"I'm on my way. I'll meet you upstairs at Bennington 8." Zander hung up without saying goodbye.

It was showtime.

Ryan checked the inside pocket of his jacket, adjusted his cuff links and smoothed his tie before he headed out. He strode down the hall on his way to the elevator and cast a quick glance at the sitting area in the lobby. It was empty, just as it had been for nearly a week. Once Evangeline had moved into his apartment, he'd issued a new mandate—the hotel lobby was for guests only.

No more bachelorettes.

They were free to hang out in the jazz bar if they wanted, but after a few days without a Ryan Wilde sighting, they'd given up. At least he'd gotten something right.

He seized on to this thought as he stepped onto the elevator, clung to it as he climbed closer to the restaurant. With each passing second, the night was coming closer to an end. But when the elevator doors swished open and he made his way to the snow-swept atrium that was Bennington 8, a chill came over him. He didn't need anyone to tell him what had happened, because he sensed her absence. He already knew.

Evangeline had left the building.

Chapter Fifteen

"I thought you said she was all in." Zander's panicked gaze shot back and forth across the elegant restaurant, searching for Evangeline.

He could look all he wanted. She wasn't there. Ryan had checked. "I did say that."

All in.

She'd promised to stay and make the night with Carlo Bocci a success. She'd given him her word.

He'd hurt her. He knew that. God, how he knew it. But he couldn't believe she'd gone. Minutes ago, she'd been in his office, talking about selecting wine for Bocci's meal. What had happened?

No one at Bennington 8 had seen her. Not the maître d'. Not the bartender. None of the servers. Which meant she hadn't ever gone to the restaurant floor at all. She'd simply walked out of his office and left.

"Then where is she?" Zander said through gritted teeth.

Ryan cut his cousin a sideways glance. "Not now."

Zander did a double take. "Not now? Seriously? Carlo Bocci has about an inch left of his gin and tonic. In less than ten minutes, he'll be seated at the best table we've got, waiting for a sommelier who just went AWOL. If not now, then when?"

At first, Ryan didn't respond. He didn't trust himself to speak without saying something he'd later regret. Zander wasn't just his cousin. He was his oldest friend, the brother he never had. In some ways, he'd even become a father figure. The paternity test had been his way of protecting Ryan.

"She found it," he finally said in a voice as calm as he could manage.

"What are you talking about?" Zander was still standing with his arms crossed, looking out over the restaurant floor, shooting surreptitious glances toward the bar whenever possible. But a few seconds later, his face fell.

He turned his back to the restaurant and faced Ryan. "Wait a minute. Do you mean the test I gave you a few days ago?"

Ryan nodded wordlessly.

"When?"

"About a minute before Carlo Bocci checked in for his reservation. It fell out of one of my jacket pockets. She has no idea where it came from."

Zander sighed. "I'm sorry. I'll talk to her. I'll explain everything."

"That's going to be difficult, considering we have no idea where she is." He didn't allow himself to consider the possibility that she'd gone back to his apartment to collect her things and take Olive and Bee elsewhere. He was almost afraid to go home, in case he walked into an empty penthouse.

Damn it.

This was what he'd been worried about all along. She was so scared of ending up like her parents that she'd been looking for a reason to run. And he'd given her one.

"I was going to ask her to marry me tonight."

He hadn't planned on saying those words out loud, but there they were, hanging between him and Zander like a breath of cold winter air.

Zander cleared his throat, but Ryan couldn't look at him. He'd bared enough of his soul already.

"Maybe you still can." There was an unmistakable smile in Zander's voice, which told Ryan that he had no idea how upset Evangeline had been. But then he added, "Your bride just walked through the door."

Ryan spun around, and there she was—striding across the room with a bottle of wine in her hands. At first he thought he must have made a mistake. She'd been there all along, and somehow he hadn't seen her. But that couldn't be right, because no one else had seen her either.

Then he took a closer look at the bottle in her hands, and everything suddenly made sense.

Whatever you do, don't drop it.

Evangeline tightened her grasp on the vintage bottle of red and willed her hands to stop shaking. If she dropped the bottle now, the madness of the past twenty minutes would have all been for nothing.

Tony had really pulled through. If everything turned out well tonight—if her extreme long shot managed to pay off—she was going to tell Ryan to give his driver a raise. A big one. He'd gotten her to Ryan's penthouse even faster than she'd hoped. After she'd dashed upstairs to get the bottle of wine, she'd come back down to find the car idling at the curb, pointed in the direction of the Bennington. The return trip had taken less than half the time of their initial dash across Manhattan.

Tony was a miracle worker. The unicorn of chauffeurs.

Evangeline would miss him after tonight. She'd miss a lot of things.

But she couldn't think about that now. If she did, she'd never get through the next few hours without breaking down. She was having enough difficulty keeping the tears at bay already.

Ryan's presence certainly wasn't helping. He and Zander were standing in the far corner of the dining room, just outside the door to the restaurant's kitchen. Did they honestly think they were being discreet?

Actually, they were. Carlo Bocci probably wouldn't even notice them. Evangeline, however, was consciously aware of their presence. Ryan's, especially. He'd honed in on her with his gaze mere seconds after she'd crossed the threshold. The look on his face was so bewildered, so full of raw hope that she'd had to look away.

If he thought she was doing this for him, he was only partially right. She was also doing it for herself. And for her unborn baby. It was time to say goodbye to the past, once and for all.

"Mr. Bocci has been seated at table twenty-five. He's using the alias Mark Spencer," the maître d' said as he met her halfway across the room.

"Perfect. I have his selection ready."

The maître d' cast a wary glance at the bottle. "You're not going to ask him what kind of wine he'd prefer? Or give him a chance to go over the list you've been working on for weeks?"

"No." She shook her head. "It's this one."

It was one of a kind—the only vintage like it in existence. What more could he possibly want?

"All right, then. You're the expert. I think he's ready."

Evangeline took a deep breath. "Here we go."

Bocci sat with his back to her as she approached. Unfortunately, Ryan and Zander were situated on the exact opposite side of the room, making them impossible to ignore. She dropped her gaze to the floor and tried her best to focus on the elegant pattern of the black-and-white marble tile beneath her feet, but it was no use. She couldn't help but look at Ryan. After this evening, she wouldn't get to see him like this again.

She'd never keep his baby from him. If he had any interest in seeing the child or being involved in the baby's life, they'd work something out. She'd see him on alternating weekends when they traded diaper bags and strollers and she pretended that she'd never once believed that the three of them could live happily-ever-after.

But she'd never see him look at her the way he was regarding her now—as if she were the most beautiful woman he'd ever set eyes on.

She bit down on the inside of her cheek to keep from crying. It didn't matter if he thought she was beautiful. Nor did it matter if he thought he loved her. She knew the truth now. He didn't trust her. Grandpa Bob insisted she'd know love when she saw it, and while she still wasn't altogether convinced that she would, she knew that love and trust were intertwined. You couldn't have one without the other.

As she slowed to a stop beside Bocci's table, Ryan mouthed something to her.

You don't have to do this.

But she did. She wanted to.

"Mr. Spencer, welcome to Bennington 8." She gave herself a mental pat on the back for remembering to use Bocci's fake name. After all, they weren't supposed to know it was him.

"Thank you." He glanced up from the menu in his hands, and his gaze snagged on the wine bottle. A frown tugged at the corner of his mouth.

Maybe this was a crazy idea, after all.

Too late.

"My name is Evangeline Holly, and I'm the hotel's sommelier." She presented the bottle on his right side, as proper wine etiquette dictated. "I'd like to recommend a very special vintage tonight, a rare and unique opportunity to experience a one-of-a-kind wine."

He lifted a dubious brow. "One of a kind? How so?"

"This wine is a cabernet franc from Chateau Holly in New York's Finger Lakes region. The vineyard ceased operations more than twenty years ago, and this is its last remaining bottle. It's a rich wine, aged to perfection, with notes of tart berries, cedar and warm toast." She smiled, and from some forgotten place deep inside, a tiny spark of pride flickered to life.

The bottle in her hands represented her heritage. Her parents had given her more than brokenness. They'd gifted her with a passion for wine and its history—her life's work. Someday she'd pass it along to her own child. Her baby wouldn't know what it was like to grow up and eat grapes fresh from the vine, but she'd teach her child other things—how to identify a fine Bordeaux, how sipping a good wine was the best way to slow down and experience a moment, how loving wine was an exercise in appreciation.

"I see." Bocci scanned the label. His face was a blank slate, but at least his frown had disappeared. "This is highly unusual."

"As I said…" Her smile widened. "This is a rare and special opportunity. If you'd prefer something else, I'd be happy to show you our house wine list."

She held her breath while he took another look at the label.

"I usually prefer old-world wines." He looked up, and she thought she spied a trace of a smile in his eyes. "But you've won me over with your confidence. I'll give it a try."

"Excellent." She pulled her sommelier knife from the pocket of her fitted blazer and used it to score the foil around the top of the bottle, being careful not to let the bottle come in contact with the table.

During a proper wine presentation, nothing in the sommelier's hands should touch the tabletop. Not even the wine itself. It could be something of a juggling act. Evangeline preferred to think of it as a dance.

She removed the loosened foil top and slipped it into her pocket, along with the knife. Then she pulled out her corkscrew and inserted it into the center of the cork.

Please don't be rotten.

This wine was old. She'd done her best to store it properly, but it wasn't as if the bottle had been sitting in a climate-controlled cellar for two decades. Recommending a wine she'd never actually sampled as an adult was risky enough without the added chance of a crumbly, dried-out cork. If the cork fell apart into the bottle of wine before she could remove it, Bennington 8 could kiss its Michelin star goodbye.

For once in Evangeline's life, fate was on her side. The cork slid out as smooth as butter.

She handed it to Bocci for his inspection. The underside of the cork was wet, just as it should be. He nodded his approval.

By some miracle, her hands didn't shake as she poured a small amount into a wineglass. Nor did she recoil at the wine's bouquet. She could smell the berries—plump red cherries and crushed raspberries, the kind just ripe enough for making jam. She could smell the cedar, too, balsamic and smoky.

She didn't even need to taste the wine to know it would be good.

No, not good.

It would be perfect.

Bocci tasted the sample sip she poured for him, and she could tell the moment that the wine touched his tongue. His eyes widened in surprise and he lifted his gaze to hers.

"Miss Holly, I'm stunned to tell you that this is the best wine I've ever tasted."

Three stars.

At the end of his meal, Carlo Bocci had walked right up to Ryan and Zander, revealed himself to be the Michelin reviewer and announced that he'd be awarding Bennington 8 the highest ranking possible—three coveted Michelin stars. There were only a dozen other three-starred restaurants in America. Bennington 8 would now go down in history as one of the best of the best.

It was more than they'd dared to hope for.

And all because of Evangeline.

Ryan wanted to sweep her off of her feet and twirl her around until she tossed her head back and laughed. He wanted to kiss her full on the lips right there in front of everyone who'd stayed for the impromptu victory party at the Bennington bar. Then he wanted to take her home and make love to her until the sun came up.

But he couldn't do any of those things, because she was in the middle of packing up her things—her champagne saber, the port tongs she'd used during her interview, the now-empty wine bottle from Chateau Holly. They were all neatly tucked away in her bag. The message was clear.

She wasn't coming back.

She'd kept her promise. She'd stayed until Bocci paid them a visit. She'd knocked it out of the park, and now she was done.

They were done.

Ryan took a deep breath. *Not if I can help it.*

"You're not just going to stand here and let her leave without telling her how you feel, are you?" Zander said under his breath as he sipped his champagne. Dom Pérignon. They were in the big leagues now.

"Absolutely not." He was going to do more than just tell her. He was also going to show her…in the best way he knew how.

"I didn't think so." Zander gave him a firm pat on the back. "Go get her."

He set his champagne glass down on the bar and walked to the table by the wine cooler where she was slipping one last thing into her bag. A cork.

"Is that from tonight's bottle?" he asked.

She looked up and smiled, but the glimmer in her eyes was bittersweet. "Yes."

She toyed with the cork, rolling it back and forth with her fingertips. It took great effort on Ryan's part not to stare. The thought of never kissing those hands, never seeing them cradle their newborn baby, was killing him.

His voice dropped an octave. "Why did you do it? That bottle of wine meant the world to you."

"It was time to let it go. Not just the wine, but all of it. I don't want to bring a baby into the world who I'm afraid to love. I want to be the best mother I can possibly be." Her bottom lip began to quiver. "The other night, my grandpa told me that love looked a lot like sacrifice. I wanted to make that sacrifice—for you, and for our baby."

She loved him.

She hadn't said it, but she did. That knowledge

should have made him happy, but the light in her eyes had dimmed on those last two words.

Our baby.

"The baby is yours, Ryan. I wish you believed me, but I understand why you don't. If you want me to take the paternity test, I will." Her eyes grew shiny with tears. Two bottomless pools of blue. "Either way, it's over between us. I know you think you love me, but this isn't love."

"Yes, it is. Eve, I've loved you since the night I met you. You pulled me straight out of my past and into the present. You saved me. Can't you see that? I hadn't so much as looked at a woman in over a year until I saw you in that wine bar, wielding that butcher knife like some kind of ninja wine goddess. I wanted you then, but I want you more now. I want forever with you." He blew out a breath. "And as for that test... I didn't have anything to do with it. Zander gave it to me, because he thought I needed proof. I don't. I'm ready to leave the past behind and start a new life with you and our baby. *Our* child. I told Zander I didn't need proof almost a week ago. He's standing right over there if you'd like to confirm it."

She blinked, and a tear slipped down her cheek. The cork in her hands fell to the floor. Neither one of them bothered to pick it up. "Is that true?"

"Yes but, I'm not finished. I didn't go to Chicago last night. I went somewhere else." He wished he could have avoided lying, but he'd wanted to surprise her. It seemed insignificant at the time, back when the trust between them wasn't so fragile.

But maybe it was better this way. Maybe this was the only way to move forward. As one.

"I don't understand. Where did you go?"

He reached into the inside pocket of his jacket and pulled out an envelope. "I went to the Finger Lakes region. To a little place near Cayuga Lake, where the soil is supposed to be perfect for growing grapes. The land hasn't been tilled in years, but it seems like just the place for a new beginning...just the place to start a family."

He reached for her wrist, turned her hand over and set the envelope gently in her palm. "Open it."

She took a deep breath and slid a finger beneath the envelope's flap, breaking the seal. A slow smile came to her lips as she unfolded the contents, and then all at once, her face broke into a beatific grin. "This is a deed. You *bought* a vineyard?"

"Love, it's not just a vineyard. It's your vineyard. It's the exact parcel of land where Chateau Holly was located. I got the information from your bottle's label and tracked down the owner." Purchasing the land had been the easy part. If they were going to turn it into a working vineyard, they had a lot of work to do. If Evangeline just wanted to hold on to it and let it stay as it was, that was fine, too. He just wanted to give her back a piece of her childhood. The piece she loved most.

"I can't believe you did this." She couldn't stop staring at the deed.

When she finally looked up, he was no longer standing beside her. He'd dropped down to one knee. The paper in Evangeline's hand fluttered to the floor, alongside the confetti that had been tossed around while the champagne was being poured—tiny gold stars.

And there, with stars scattered at her feet and their baby growing inside her, Ryan Wilde asked Evangeline Holly to be his wife.

Her answer was an unequivocal yes.

Epilogue

One year later

Evangeline sat near the head of a rustic farm table that had been placed between two rows of grapevines located in the most scenic portion of the vineyard. The farm table had been her husband's idea, and it had been a good one. It was made of repurposed wood, perfect for a harvest party. Even more perfect for celebrating a place where they'd made something beautiful out of the discarded remains of the past.

The table was set for ten. All the family was present—Tessa and Julian, Allegra and Zander, Chloe, Emily, Grandpa Bob. Even Olive and Bee were there, snoozing in a dog bed that Julian had made out of a sawed-off wine barrel stuffed with a generous amount of cushions. And of course Ryan was there, too. He stood beside Evangeline, holding their daughter in the crook of his arm and raising a glass in a toast.

"Eve and I want to thank you all for coming out here today to celebrate the first vintage from Wilde Hearts Winery." He grinned down at her.

In the beginning, once plans for the wedding had been made and after Evangeline's morning sickness had passed, they'd been stumped as to what to name the vineyard. Ryan insisted he'd be fine with calling it Chateau Holly. But Evangeline wasn't. The winery represented a new beginning, so it needed a new name.

Choosing a name for their daughter had been far easier. Holly Wilde was the obvious choice, and they both loved it. Boom. Done.

Naming the vineyard was a far more difficult task, until their wedding night when Ryan finished unbuttoning Evangeline from her wedding dress and groaned as it fell to the floor in a puff of white tulle.

Be still my Wilde heart.

The second he'd uttered those words, she knew they'd found a name.

No one knew the story of how they'd come up with it. It was their little secret.

"We couldn't have pulled off the challenging feat of getting this vineyard off the ground without each and every one of you," Ryan continued.

"I'll drink to that," Zander said wryly.

Allegra gave him a playful swat. "Let the man finish his toast. I'm ready to sample this wine."

It was their first bottle from their very first barrel—a cabernet franc, just like the vintage Evangeline had poured for Carlo Bocci a year ago. Ryan kept suggesting they create a pinot grigio instead. He was joking, obviously.

Evangeline hoped he was, anyway.

"I also want to congratulate my beautiful wife for recently passing her Certified Sommelier exam." Ryan lifted his glass a little higher and shot her a wink.

"Hear, hear!" Grandpa Bob said. He'd been spending weekends at the vineyard, away from his assisted living facility, and seemed to be getting some of his old spunk back.

"This doesn't mean you're going to give us a long description of what this wine is supposed to taste like before we're allowed to take a sip, does it?" Julian stared into his glass.

"No." Evangeline shook her head. "It means Zander is going to let me keep working at Bennington 8."

"Nonsense. The three Michelin stars negated that whole condition. Surely I told you that." He frowned.

"You didn't, actually. But I would have gone through the certification anyway, if it makes you feel any better."

"It does." Zander arched a brow and cut his gaze toward Ryan. "Although what would really make me feel better is if your husband would finish his lengthy toast and let us drink."

Holly let out a happy squeal.

Evangeline stood to hand her little girl her favorite stuffed toy and wrap her arms around Ryan's waist. "I hate to tell you this, but it sounds like even your daughter wants you to wrap this up."

"Her wish is my command." Ryan brushed a tender kiss to the top of Holly's head. "Cheers, everyone! To the harvest!"

"To the harvest," they all echoed.

Glasses clinked all around, and a breeze blew through the valley, rustling the grapevines. The air grew heavy with the lush perfume of good wine, good grapes and good people. Family.

Drunk on happiness, Evangeline rose to her tiptoes and pressed her lips to Ryan's ear, to the sensitive, secret spot she knew so well.

"And to you, my handsome husband," she whispered. "Be still my Wilde heart."

* * * * *

LET'S TALK
Romance

For exclusive extracts, competitions
and special offers, find us online:

- **f** facebook.com/millsandboon
- 🐦 @MillsandBoon
- 📷 @MillsandBoonUK

Get in touch on 01413 063232

For all the latest titles coming soon, visit
millsandboon.co.uk/nextmonth

MILLS & BOON
MODERN
Power and Passion

Prepare to be swept off your feet by sophisticated, sexy and seductive heroes, in some of the world's most glamourous and romantic locations, where power and passion collide.

MILLS & BOON
True Love
Romance from the Heart

Celebrate true love with tender stories of heartfelt romance, from the rush of falling in love to the joy a new baby can bring, and a focus on the emotional heart of a relationship.

MILLS & BOON
Desire

Indulge in secrets and scandal, intense drama and plenty of sizzling hot action with powerful and passionate heroes who have it all: wealth, status, good looks…everything but the right woman.

JOIN US ON SOCIAL MEDIA!

Stay up to date with our latest releases, author news and gossip, special offers and discounts, and all the behind-the-scenes action from Mills & Boon...

 millsandboon

 millsandboonuk

 millsandboon

It might just be true love...